MW00978718

Six Positions

.....

Six Positions

Sex Writing
by Andy Quan

Green Candy Press

SIX POSTIONS: *Sex Writing*
by Andy Quan
ISBN 1-931160-36-8

Published by Green Candy Press, www.greencandypress.com

Design: Ian Phillips
Cover photography: Copyright © Tony Fong
Previous publication histories on page 208.

Some proper names and details have been changed in the autobiographical pieces in this book to protect the privacy of living individuals.

Printed in Canada by Transcontinental Printing Inc.
Massively Distributed by P.G.W.

•••••

To Daniel, Frank, Trevor and David

. . . . .

Contents

. . . . .

At First Sight

Love is a four letter word. We use it to curse, to draw attention to ourselves, to be cool. We wrap our lips around it to feel its power. I've never had much use for it, since I don't see the point in cursing or drawing attention to myself.

Plus all the jabber-jabber I hear from my friends. I mean, look at Gary: perfectly presentable, nice guy, good job, no spectacular childhood trauma or kooky family history; you'd think he'd have his head screwed on right. But no, he walks around with this big gaping hole in the side of his body that says, "want, want." Flops around like a fish on dry land.

He's waiting for Romeo, or Julio, or someone, but won't go out looking for him, gets himself caught up in work, too scared to be set up on dates; spends time with the same old friends, or takes care of his nephews on weekends. Too often, I think. All the time wanting this house to crash down upon him, as if from the tornado in *The Wizard of Oz*. Plop. The house of love.

But active searching hasn't helped my other friend, Albert. He's not actually a friend, I guess, but he hangs around Matthew, my ex-boyfriend, so much we end up drinking at the same bar. Albert has joined about every organization in the city, making himself available. Almost drowned trying out for the gay water polo team. Sang through five seasons of the gay men's chorus. Faked his way into the gay professionals' group by borrowing Matthew's Hugo Boss suits. Dinner clubs, activist gatherings, that new age meditation group—he's tried it all. I think it's the neon sign above his head that scares people off.

Why can't people learn to be single? I've always thought. Learn to live with yourself, sleep on whatever side of the bed pleases you, jack off when you want. Come and go as you please. I know they bitch about me behind my back, whether from love or jealousy. "He never seems to be interested in finding someone. Probably spends too much time at sex clubs and saunas."

It's a bank holiday weekend, bless the god of four-day work-weeks. All the queens in the town are deciding what to do, which big party to go to. I'm opting for Famous Five: huge space, tons of boys down to London for the weekend, five different DJs and dance clubs, that's where it gets its name. I've never been and I hear that it's going downhill. They better come up with a new gimmick before they crash and burn, yesterday's news. The cops don't help the ambience either. Last time, one friend was caught with five tabs of E and hauled off to the station. His boyfriend, already high, spent the next five hours decorating the dance floor with tears, the light show in each room beamed onto his wet, shiny face. They're probably not going tonight, but I will.

Stroke of midnight, I arrive just after. I only have one lager and a quick shuffle on the dance floor to "Everybody's Free."

Andy Quan

. . . . .

When are they going to stop playing that song? They start playing the dance remix to that *Titanic* theme song, I run into another section, and they start playing it there too.

So here I am in the darkroom in the bottommost club. Like a homing pigeon, I zeroed in closer and closer, saw pre- and post-coital facial expressions, sweat and flesh, and clusters of men in that stance they do against the wall outside of darkrooms.

I jump in right away. I never hesitated before diving into swimming pools either. It's like one big swim team, dozens of men, some huddled into each other as if listening to the coach's rallying speech before the race begins. Competitors and teammates, tall and short, some stretching down on the floor, others bent over like they're at the starting block, a few stretching up and to the side. Others casual, pacing around.

Stepping over this cluster, I recognize this guy I'd seen upstairs, a model type, straight out of the pages of a fitness magazine. He's blowing this broad-shouldered Asian guy, a bit chunky around the midsection, who's tongue-kissing this skinny redhead who looks about sixteen. The equality of flesh and desire. Unexpected pairings.

I strip off my shirt in the glowing darkness: a single exit sign in the corner throws a red blanket over all of us. I can feel the pockets of energy forming, whipping into frenzies in different corners. I easily glide towards the warmth, through the packed crowd. Faced away, I feel smooth wide backs against my chest and stomach; faced towards me, round pectorals, nipples, front corners of biceps, meaty forearms. I free my hands from their cages, let them roam through the space in front of me; feel the outline of torsos and their warm sweat; cup and squeeze balls, this one a plum, that one a large avocado. I lift, grab, stroke, pull cocks, short and fat, long and thin, long and fat.

Yin and yang in the corner, these couple of guys, one black and tall, gleaming white teeth, muscular but in a way you can sink into it, fingers press and bounce into that athleticism. His cock like a flagpole extending out of tight curly pubic hair. It's thick and fleshy, like the rotating round of meat in Lebanese shawarma restaurants.

Whitey is shorter and pale, thin lips, you can't see his teeth, his mouth is closed but smiling. He's taut and lean, maybe one of those guys who dance each weekend straight through on ecstasy, twenty-four hours, thirty-six, drinking only water, the calories fly off, the fat disappears. Strip the shirt off like bandages from a plastic surgery patient. It's like a topographic map, rivers and valleys, blue veins, beautiful beautiful lines, higher elevations that you want to explore. His cock is thinner, long, hard and tight like his skin; it's like a pen you want to grab to write that novel you've always thought you had inside you.

They look at me, I return the glance, this triangle of desire closes and suddenly we're kissing, all three of us at the same time, heads in close, our tongues in and out. A three-note chord sounds over our heads; percussive moans and rhythms make it dance.

It's at this very moment, from the corner of my eye, I see him next to us, with another guy. Not even see him, really, but just a flash of dark eyes, a glimmer of darkness inside of his mouth before his lips connect with flesh and travel down a body and out of sight.

Now, my trio is moving in rhythm, we're backup singers swinging in perfect time, it's doo-wap-a-shoo-bop, one down, two up, two down, one up; my face in an armpit, the crevice of a chest, between two legs, between four legs, surrounded in dark warmth between two bodies; a pulsing womb.

I rise up as if out of water, and I'm filled with love, my heart is ticker-taping messages to the crowd. The guy I spotted earlier and his partner have moved closer, my couple notices as well, and then we're five, a surging ball of energy, perspiration and limbs, a flock of orifices, a herd of phalli. The tongues are hard and soft and quick and slow, and in between hot black breaths, and not being able to think at all, lost in ecstasy, I notice him, onyx eyes and shaved head, noticing me.

I like the way he gives pleasure to the others, the mischievous smile of it all, playful but tough. His generosity too, taking a ripe cock between his lips, and then offering it to me; we start to kiss as we reach to lick the same nipple. Notice our simultaneous, similar desire.

As if a whole ocean has drained out of our bodies, the tide going out, we come into consciousness, an awareness of people around us. We stand facing each other, the others have left, and I faintly recall their murmured farewells. Goodbye. Thanks. Ta. Ciao.

He takes my hand, leads me out the door. Love at first sight, forever.

.....

Instrumental

FLUTE

Jonathan was a flautist. He hypnotized me. Somehow, as the orchestra played, and the soft glint from the lights above reflected along the length of his polished silver flute, I was transfixed. Waited for him after the performance. Until he came out of the dressing room hall, still in formal tuxedo, and paused in front of me. I followed the colors from his chin to shoulder: pink, white, black. Those stripes of formality have always made me weak.

I could see right away how strong his lips were, holding back a torrent of breath that when released became bright melody. In a soft light, I could see the shape of his lips pursing, the muscles around the mouth tensing and moving forward. Suddenly, I was caught in a gust of wind. I was floating in the air, notes and melodies vibrating out of my bones and skin. The air around me warm. Cool. Moist like the leaves of a fern after a sudden morning rain.

He played every part of me that night: arms and legs, the edge of my ear, each finger, my Adam's apple. The pressure of the air would pulse, strengthen and ease. The stream of air would widen so I felt I could jump and bounce off it like a trampoline. Then narrow like a spotlight into a finger, a match, a needle. A thousand needles and me so perfectly balanced upon them that I remained unpierced. Whole.

CONDUCTOR

They are musicians but are separate from the others. *The conductor.* Far and few between. They have music inside of them, but rather than express it through a single vessel, they learn to control it. Maybe they had already gained a respectable expertise in another instrument: piano certainly, violin? Or maybe they came to it directly, a vocation called to them in their sleep. Their arms and wrists danced at night. They awoke with sore muscles, and could not explain why.

Nick found other conductors stuffy. He could go toe-to-toe with them talking about the works of a specific composer, the greatest symphonies, obscure Italian operas. He loved his work. He knew that he would be as good as or better than the rest of his classmates.

But rather than coming from a long line of conductors, or even a family of musicians, Nick had come from a working-class family. His father sold industrial deep fryers to cafés and roadside diners. His mother brought in a tidy additional income through clothes repairs and alterations. Nick's dream of conducting (which he believed had fallen upon him like pollen in his first days of existence) had been fired by seeing Mickey Mouse with a baton pulling up oceans and teasing out stars in Walt Disney's *Fantasia*. He can still remember his left foot sticking to spilt soda pop on the dirty cinema floor, the smell of popcorn everywhere, tattered seats, and the dusty dark. Looking up and seeing his future ahead of him.

He's never told anyone that. And it's not his only secret.

What he *never* tells his colleagues is of his passion for punk music. Thrash. Hard-core speedy guitars. Loud jarring sounds that enter your head in dark shapes, or flashes of light. He attends concerts when he can, dresses simply in T-shirt and jeans, and slips into the crowd, strikes up conversations with other aficionados.

What he *sometimes* does not tell his colleagues is of his late evenings in bars and discos, scanning a crowd, deciding whether or not to take someone home or go to theirs. Rather like choosing between conducting your own symphony or doing a guest spot in another town. Depending on the mood.

I was in awe of him from the beginning, not something I'd felt for others and certainly, not people I'd met in bars. *In awe.* But that's what I felt, without understanding why. He appeared from out of the crowd. I felt his command.

Do the players in the orchestra feel this as well? This mastery. A conductor needs to gain the respect of each one of his musicians, through skill and instinct, like a mass hypnotist, or the leader of a cult. The methods: the right tone of voice, showing respect to more influential musicians, pressure where it is needed, coercion if necessary. It's not a simple difference between the ability to play a piccolo and one to play timpani. This command.

But power is not ever as simple or as crude as people think. Those truly in authority make it look easy. Small gestures. *I'm only doing my job.* Meanwhile, the ship sails beneath them, the grid of traffic flows, the army marches,

.....

and the band plays on.

"What do you feel like doing?" he asked.

The nightclub shifted a full beat out of focus. I felt winded suddenly, as if arriving at the top of a flight of stairs. "Anything you want," I replied.

He'd removed his shoes and socks, pants and underwear. But had left his shirt on, which was long sleeved and of a thin expensive cotton. Buttons undone from neck to waist, also at the wrists. He leaned forward and swayed. His shirt fell away from him and exposed his torso. Covering, uncovering. He appeared more naked this way than if he actually had been.

We touched, as if I was the concertmaster, the first violinist, the person who gets to shake his hand before the concert begins. When we kissed, it was formal but passionate, arms at tight angles, and backs kept straight. Five or ten minutes only, then he pulled away.

Most of the time, he stood and the energy was concentrated in his arms and his hands. I moved from in front of him to the bed, back and forth, I roamed around his unfamiliar bedroom. Most of the time, we did not actually touch, but watched each other instead, the rhythm of blood flowing, our erections surging or ebbing, sweat forming and drying on our bodies.

There was no audience, though there might have been. I gave the performance of my life. Like I had a hundred voices capable of making thousands of sounds. All the parts of my body working together, perfectly, at once. Creating music, but in a way that I did not completely understand. I could feel the graceful arc of the violinist's bow, the propelling motion of the right arm pushing air in a ribbon across my face. The thick excited gurgling of the timpani at the base of my spine. The old dignified strains of a cello weaving through my ribs. The warm spit of the French horn player collecting at the back of my throat.

There was no intermission, we played right through, and when both he and I and the imaginary audience had had our fill, he slowly bent his torso down towards the ground. Then rose and walked towards me, letting his shirt slip off and dangle in midair.

I slept that night with his arms wrapped around me, his hands, for once, stilled.

BASS

You know the bass guitarist. Just out of the spotlight, hiding in the half-light at the back of the stage, a calm eddy in a rushing river, an indentation in a cliff face where the wind doesn't reach. The drummer on one side, arms multiplying like an Indian goddess; on the other, the octopus fingers of the pianist splaying through sea air; saxophonist center stage right, a brass fury of horn and sweetness; center stage vocalist playing huge sporting games with energy and sound, taking it in, giving it all away.

Amidst all that: him, feet less than shoulder width apart, a slight rock from time to time sliding into a sway. The legs and hips are toothpicks. The torso is a carriage. The shoulders lean forward to create a space below, they fall back to lift the infant into a cradle. Just awoken, his yowl turns into a hum. The arms are mismatched socks. The right arm is tightly tucked against the body, a chicken foot, a claw. It reaches under the round thigh of the bass and grabs and plucks and

.....

strokes the dark center. If it was pubic hair instead of electric cord, it would be braided by now, unbraided, curled, frizzed, straightened, gelled, spiked, waxed, bleached and colored. A body wave for good measure. The left arm falls down, crooks up into a *V.* The fingers are the long legs of a dancing spider or a crane fly skipping across a pond in the middle of a yellow-green glade, tall grasses, pollen in the air; you sneeze and the insect skitters. A saunter turns into a sprint.

Above this activity, the head is passive, a fixed globe, a longitudinal smile, a gentle curve that doesn't quite break into a grin. He's not showy; if he wanted the attention he'd have taken up a different instrument. But it's he who has the power, and no one knows it, not even the other musicians. They're carrying on; he's carrying it all. He's the railroad tracks beneath their train, the rope stretched tight beneath their stride and flips. Do all the acrobatics they want, humans still can't fly. He knows this.

The short scales, fourths and fifths, chromatic drops, back to the tonic. He's there, he's under them, he keeps it moving. If he stopped, the audience would know something was missing. They wouldn't know what it was.

He's like this in bed too. He doesn't look like he's doing much. Yeah, he seems to be enjoying himself, his foot tapping time, the upward turn of his mouth. Then suddenly this vibration fills up your mind with runs and scales and intervals, and he's playing you like strings. Your body is taken over in pleasure and it's not your own.

Boom boom boom. This is dry sex; if it was any wetter, you might get electrocuted. As it is, there's a crackle in the air, feedback and circuit clicks up and down the length of you.

He reaches over. He's getting into the groove. But first things first. Here he stops, he's tuning you up at the base of your torso, at the place where your legs meet, at your groin. You've got to twist and turn and loosen so that the pitch falls into place just so, so that all the strings are sounding off the same vibrations. This is what he's doing, bringing you further and further into pleasure, his ear on your stomach. *Ping!* Sharper, sharper, that's it. *Ping!* Now, that one's too sharp, bring it down, flatten it out. His breath warms your skin like a soft wind coming up on the desert outback. He's playing your nipples, the folds of skin near your armpit, the bounce in the muscles in your chest, the waves of your abdomen. He's bringing it all into tune.

SAXOPHONE

I'd thought of a saxophone player as flexible, easy, groovy. Improvisational. But that wasn't the case at all. What he did, he did well, but he stayed stiffly to what he knew. He played sax; he wasn't a multi-instrumentalist.

So there we were. I tried to move his hands out of position; tried to coax his body out of its slightly hunched and twisted stance. I had no luck. I gave in. He started on the smaller parts, and worked his way up. The tips of my index and middle fingers in his mouth. The top of his teeth resting just over my fingernails, his bottom lip curled up over teeth pressing up into the first segments of my fingers. His right hand above left, holding my forearm, his two thumbs balanced on one side, the fingers starting to rock and play on the other.

First one arm, then the other, both legs, his mouth on

the toes of my feet, then the whole torso, finding reeds and mouthpieces at all extremities, keys to press with his fingers. My body makes soft clicks, cavities half open and close at different pitches. His right hand always above left, thumbs trying to cradle behind, little fingers itching to press any key they can find.

I reach out to play with him as well, his long lean torso slowly covered with perspiration, a slick golden glow; my hands polish the surface.

He plays the knobs on my spine, lowers me down to the ground, and positions his mouth over my groin. It is then that I realize that the fingers are less important than the mouth, that the music all comes from there. *Embouchure* is the word for it. The way that he presses his tongue and lips around the mouthpiece and reed, the exact configuration of the muscles in his cheeks and mouth, the way he blows, the way he brings the instrument to life, the way he makes love.

Blow. Blow. Blow me.

Sounds come out of my ears and nostrils. All the pores of my skin.

PIANO

He was kicked out of the academy after Leonard, the harpsichordist (and part-time piano tuner), broke down in tears in the master's office. In front of the assembled authorities, he confessed that he'd been forced into it, that it was not his fault, and that yes, he did it, but can't you see, Patrick was "too forceful, too persuasive, too threatening, too too too." His speech suddenly lost meaning and turned into musical sounds.

.....

Faced with the blubbering mess in front of them, and unwilling to expel a student they knew would go on to great things (as Leonard did, during his three record deal with Deutsche Grammophon, reinterpreting the rediscovered seventeenth-century Italian composer, Fabiolini. Fugues for five hands. Preludes in the key of *fa*.), the headmasters instead (gleefully) took the opportunity to bid adieu (insincerely) to Patrick whose talents they'd failed to recognize.

No matter. Patrick really had to admit that blackmailing Leonard into retuning the academy's priceless Bosendorfer to the seventeen tone scale of Kazakhstan throat-singers was worth the punishment, and besides he never could handle all that classical shit. Years later, he'd grin cheekily at the memory, pleased at his skill, that he had found Leonard's weak spot. Though Leonard was afraid of his own body, and more so of his desires being discovered, Patrick had firstly seduced and secondly explored Leonard's young nervous body until he found the hairless soft wrinkled folds of skin between Leonard's anus and scrotum. He experimented from gentle tonguing to hungry devouring and found that the optimum technique was somewhere in between. Patrick thought of the action as the sharp vocal intake of breath you make when you see someone you really really want to fuck. Applied to Leonard, it would send him into a different world. Patrick wondered if Leonard had found people in later life who had let him go back there.

Patrick developed his classical repertoire regardless, could pick out pop and folk tunes easily, and was much amused by house music. Still, it was as a jazz player that Patrick was in demand. He would choose only the most glamorous, young, up-and-coming singers, and if chosen by him, they knew their careers were set into ascendancy. He would match his playing to their voices like a master choosing frames for a Renaissance painting.

Then, during his piano solos, he would steal the attention. He would become the painting and they were simply the frames, as he exploded into color and movement, as if brushing music onto a canvas of air.

Effortlessly, he told stories of swelling emotion, lost loves and broken dreams. Even though he had never lost a love, nor had a dream dashed to the ground. No matter. That's what a virtuoso is—a conduit for something, someone, somewhere much much bigger than the instrument itself, the player or the channel.

When we met, it was like the tiniest music, sparse notes from a music box, a child's melody with too much empty space in between. Later, he said he was getting to know me, and never let anyone in too quickly.

The next was scales. Arpeggios. Octaves. Hanon finger exercises. Who would have thought that a virtuoso needs to do the basics? Formula scales. First, both hands travel up two octaves together, then separate like wings until they are four octaves apart. They come together once more, climb two and descend two, part and rejoin, and fall back down to the beginning. Up and down. Up and down, that's what we did. Elevators. Escalators. Takeoffs and landings.

He was testing me. He told me only when it was clear I had passed. Like a doctor trying out each joint, a full physical examination. Here, he scrutinized tone and texture, age, sonority, action of the keys and the type of wood I'd been made with. What kind of hall I was suited for: long and flat, or tall and round with a cupola in the ceiling.

He gave me lessons. I had stopped them when I was a teenager, as an act of rebellion against my parents. I was slow at the beginning, but there was memory left in my fingers.

"Not just the fingers," he scolded. "It's so much more than that."

His aim was to play around, expand our repertoire, see if we could do a few duets, maybe some public performance; see what it would be like if he accompanied me, or if I accompanied him.

He explained that the art of playing is to share, that music is not meant for one set of ears: a few is OK, but more is better. That means that each time music is more than practice, it is an event, an occasion, everything is to be remembered, every detail is to stand out. It is memory as well, he added. You play something like it's the first time you've heard it, the first time you've played it, and as if you are remembering the deepest emotions you've ever experienced, dark or light, and in doing so, you are making new ones.

The first time I undressed him was in a dressing room, with an unkind light glaring off a mirror in one corner. To start with, I was content with his hands and long muscular fingers. Soft palms with a touch of electricity about them. I placed his hand onto his long neck, the pronounced sky-colored veins from his wrists up the back of his hands reflecting the sinews and veins in his neck.

I lost my patience. Undid buttons, belt, zipper, shoelaces as quick as highway traffic, while he stood bemused. When I snapped down the elastic of his briefs, hands on each side pulling them straight down to his ankles, his cock stood out at a perfect straight angle, like the torso of a concert grand piano, the lid down, one long shining object with a gracious curve at the end.

I stood back to look at him and saw a person with so much energy that fat couldn't stick to him. Pleasing lines at all angles. A hairless torso, with shadings of hair down the legs, the forearms, a tidy arrangement at his groin. A scar, faded brown with a hint of white through which his appendix was removed. Prominent nipples, dark aureoles low down on the chest. I fell close to him in a long wet kiss, inside my head a jazz-inflected melody, a small French impressionist jewel from Satie or Debussy or someone whose works lay undiscovered.

The first time I fucked him: I had never stayed so long inside someone. Against the wall. On the bed. On a chair. Him on top, lowering himself onto me. Me on top, pushing his legs up to his head. On a diagonal, entering him sideways.

We paused for breath. "A music teacher at the academy called me an invert, said homosexuals bugger each other, and that is unnatural. I said, 'What is natural? Is music unnatural because it is created by men? What left in the world is still natural?' With him scowling and confused, I said, 'And your cheap shirt is not one hundred percent of any natural fiber. You'll have to get rid of that.' "

I think he told me this because he sensed that fucking was new for me, even though he made me feel like a veteran. Could he know that I had never felt so natural before, music of water and air, the tones of weather and birdsong, wind whistling through shapes of rock and of wood?

He drew me out of my reverie, shifting his ass forward and back, clenching and releasing his buttocks, a coquettish swing side to side. Suddenly it was a bawdy Slavic dance, an off-kilter ragtime, a humming kazoo solo in the middle of a Teutonic aria. Then it was rock music, seventies guitar, flesh slapping against flesh, heads thrown back and swaying. If we'd had long hair, it would have been flying every which way. We came at exactly the same time, mine inside of him, his shooting up, a perfect arc that touched my chest and fell down onto his.

The first public performance: it was at a popular gay resort with vistas of washed-out yellows and greens, and an ocean filled with small whitecaps that burst into spray. Flecks of salt on windows and woodwork.

The resort was fully occupied with gay travellers: couples, friends in pairs and threesomes, a handful of single men, all wealthy enough to escape to here and all hungry enough to want these surroundings of testosterone and chemical heat, constant cruising, tropical cocktail laughter.

Saturday evening was spent around the pool and spa, clothing optional, no one opted. Fluorescent glow-sticks lit buckets of condoms and lubricant. We staggered our entrances, wanting to warm up the audience. I strode by a row of three, my hand like a paintbrush on a fence, touching a different part of each: shoulder, chest, abdomen.

He zigzagged through couplings and threesomes, not intruding and getting involved, a light stroke down the side of someone I knew particularly pleased him, hot breath on the small of the back of another.

I beamed with pride as I watched him weave through the

gathering. He had an energy that I knew was recognized. Even without knowing why he was famous, they knew who he was.

By the time we met, all eyes were focused towards us at the center.

We performed a full symphony in dramatic E flat minor, translated to four hands, arms, legs; two tongues, cocks, assholes. *Allegro con brio* to start, fast but not too fast, to set the pace for them to follow, some watching and masturbating, some attempting imitation. *Adagio assai,* we slowed down so that all around us were deep sighs and intakes of breath. *Scherzo:* we stepped up the pace when we felt their hearts and lungs were ready for it. Dancing, dancing, in, out, up, down, side to side, all directions to build up to the finale, *allegro molto,* fast fast fast, until you reach that plane where you don't think anymore, you only feel, and what you feel is pleasure. Then, a trick to confuse the audience if they didn't know their symphonies: *poco andante,* the most tender exchange of tongues. Then *presto,* this is the fastest it gets: sweat flying in every direction, mixing with ocean salt, and the water from the whirlpool and swimming pool rising up, a mist turning into a hard cooling rain of bodies, every man you've ever wanted, slick and shining. The wind sweeps up, the sounds of palm leaves rustle together in an imitation of a great crowd. Around us everywhere, applause.

.....

First Draft

It was a lesson I was taught in a sunny classroom with brightly painted concrete walls in a quiet Vancouver neighborhood before most people in the world knew where Vancouver was. To write a report, or a letter, or basically anything important, you would do a first draft, and then a second, and then carefully recopy the whole thing onto clean paper.

I always wondered about the word *draft*. I knew it meant *wind* as well as *forcibly recruit* (I admit to precocity.) To write a draft, I imagined, was to write the wind onto a page, have it blown away into a better form and then disappear altogether.

Foolscap was another intrigue. Within the word was a stupid person and a hat. Said quickly, it was neither, and the syllables could alter to evoke *full*, *fuel*, *scape* and *cup*. So much in a silly rough bit of paper, clearly inferior to proper new lined paper glowing white, showing off three perfect holes.

So, here it is, I'm writing on whatever paper I have found but am imagining it soft and shabby as foolscap and I'm writing a first draft because really, I barely know you, so how could I draw you into finished form just yet?

First Draft

.....

This is how we met. I wrote a story. Sent it off. The editor agreed to put it in a book with other stories. You'd done the same. It was your first story published; mine as well.

The publisher had organized a night to promote the anthology where authors of these stories would do a small reading. The event was held in a small bar in Toronto, a bar that was long from back to front, but short from side to side, so when I eventually read, I would have to look far to the right and far to the left to connect with the audience.

I was in a new romance, my first one, and one that remained the most important of my romances for years ahead. Marshall arrived slightly late but managed to catch my whole reading, sitting quietly off to the left-hand side. We barely knew each other, but the quiet support he showed me that night portended well for the relationship.

It was the first time as an adult that I'd read aloud and read in front of an audience something that I'd written. I suppose as a child I had done some sort of reporting in elementary school, but I don't remember standing in front of a podium with a poem or part of a short story. That night, when I finished reading my first excerpt, the audience clapped. Since they'd not offered the same reception to the previous few readers, my head swelled and glowed. I absorbed their sounds of laughter and their response to my words.

I had read the anthology in the week previous, and without having met you, had decided that your story was my favorite. You read well, but I remember more strongly meeting you afterwards. You had a baseball cap on, wrapped around your closely shaven head, and I found myself staring into your eyes after I'd approached you and said I admired your writing and had liked your story better than the others.

You thanked me and returned the compliment. I wasn't sure if you were sincere. Someone earlier had told me how much he liked my story, and even though I wasn't sure what I thought of his, I felt compelled to say the same. Were you doing the same?

You introduced me immediately to your companion, a gesture which I mistakenly took to mean that this was someone significant, a partner or boyfriend or whatever you might have called him. But what I most remembered of that meeting was attraction. If I met you later in life, I would not know you by the distance between your brow and eyes or the angle between your lips and ears. I would know you by what I'd felt and what I hoped you felt as well, your eyes boring into me like water poured into sand.

I apologize that this story is about writers. A writer friend of mine says if he should ever write a book about writing, he'll ask his boyfriend to shoot him. I nodded enthusiastically at the time. Now I'm not so sure. I mean, here I am, recreating the described crime. I am telling you of that night when, high on accomplishment and attention, I met this writer.

If you are not another writer, (though you may be since many readers of short stories are writers of them as well) I hope that you'll transpose the experience to something more familiar. Like going to a conference and doing a presentation about something you are passionate about. Or joining up with a bunch of hobbyists, though I think that the stamp and coin collectors of yesteryear have mostly been replaced by people who are fans of certain TV shows or who dress up as large fuzzy animals.

But the analogy could be much simpler. Like when you and the kid down the street both got shiny new bicycles at the same time. You rode around, and the other kids in the neighborhood were impressed and jealous. You were happy to share the glory with someone else, the wind whistling past your ears, the smell of childhood at your nostrils.

Between the first time I met you and the next time, seven years later, I had changed from a flirtatious but relatively chaste young lad to an experienced man of the world. This is in the comparative sense. Men get to parade that. If I was a woman, I'd be considered loose and sluttish. As a man: a Romeo, Casanova, stud? Well, not really: as a gay man, similar terms apply as those applied to women, but I'll wear them loudly like a Hawaiian holiday shirt. The words *promiscuous* and *slut* along with *been around the block* and *sex-pig* instead of tropical birds and flowers.

When I see you again, I do look at your eyes, but quickly scan downwards at the more physical, and more carnal. I like what I see: a strong gym-built body, curves in all the right places. I also see that you dress as carefully as I do but probably carry it off better. I can still be a bit lazy with ironing and sometimes mix two genres without getting the right blend. You dress as hip young urban gay men do, the cut of your short sleeve shirts is flattering but not skintight, your slightly baggy shorts are of a length that reveals your strong calves below, which a colleague of mine is fixated on.

Since they've been pointed out to me, I consider them as well. They're strange things, calf muscles. Round humps pushing out from the back of our lower legs, poised solidly but awkwardly above the ankles. They point out how thin our ankles really are and the strange way our weight above balances on so little below. Some calves are barely noticeable, like a thin vase of a nondescript color. Others are hard and muscular and showy. After meeting you again, and admiring the slope and curve of yours, I start to notice them on other men. I am suddenly aware of a body part that I've never really noticed.

Another thing I found amusing about your calves is that their shapes were echoed at the top of your head. Not exactly the same curve really, but my same desire to reach over and stroke them. Your legs. Your head, closely shaven. Your hair dark but light in weight and texture, so your crown was shiny and smooth, a strong form that accentuated your handsome features.

I, on the other hand, had gone blond. It was something that I'd considered for a long time, but was deterred by the fact that I'd seen so many Asian men with odd glowing shades of orange on their heads and blond that wasn't really blond. The story, my hairdresser had revealed, was that they dyed their hair at home. A professional job, bleached carefully with an expensive toner, would result in what I wanted.

It did, a gesture that radically improved my sex life. The incongruity of an Asian with blond hair caused people to look at me more closely, and getting handsome men to look at me was certainly an advantage if I wanted to look at them.

So we stood next to each other, a dyed blond and a shaved head, and I thought there was similarity in that. We were both writers (who had stories and poems published in similar books and magazines) and I was fashioning in my mind the hopes of twinned desire, that you were attracted to me as much as I was to you. But the real twinned desire was evidenced by our hair or lack of it. A desire to be noticed by others.

I've left it behind, poetry, to write this. The sculpted form, careful placement, snappy one-liners. Instead I fall into the tumbleweeds of prose, my thoughts jammed up against each other like tenement houses. I dare to be sloppy, sloppier than poems at least.

I read your latest poems and during any stanza about the body or sex, I imagined making love with you. The poems were variable. Like me, you could slip into describing sentiment rather than evoking it. That, and a tendency to overwrite, to use a phrase too literary or pretty for the image behind it. This we share in common. "Some of the poems are very old," you'd said, handing your chapbook to me.

Unlike me, you hold back. You can tell stories in few words that allude to larger histories. Your short brushstrokes make do for a painting. When it works, it's compact and haunting. You leave the poem alone, even if you might want to stay. I explain too much. You know this already.

When I read your poems, I can't always analyze them, though I know that you've hit your mark. Sometimes, I want more narrative though, more connections between the poems themselves. I want to read twenty short prose poems about your last boyfriend and a dozen couplets about your current one. I want to insinuate myself into your skin so you write one about me.

Andy Quan

.....

We have met again at a conference. It's impossible not to meet people at conferences, but sometimes surprising when you've met them before in different lives. The first time I'd met you, I was studying political science, and you medicine. Now, we are both working with AIDS, the virus that confuses and confounds us and mutates with each replication. It is not strange that we've both been drawn into the same arena.

"Are you seeing anyone?" I'm more interested in your personal than your professional life. I ask you about the man you were with the first time we met, and realize with some embarrassment that I have revealed my desire too early.

"No, he was just a friend, never a boyfriend. I am seeing someone now. We live together." You explain that he is a schoolteacher and kind and is called Mark.

Later, I am still the interrogater. "Do you have an open relationship?"

When I came out in my early twenties and during travels to Europe soon after, I would never have asked this question. I asked instead, "Do you have a partner?" and if the answer was yes, no matter how close they sat next to me, or stared intently into my eyes, I was breezy and amiable but gave no encouragement, nor understood that some may have been given. Monogamy was the only model I'd heard about and if someone was attached, it meant they weren't available to me.

Actually, I might have asked "Do you have diplomatic immunity?" A joke that I pretend I made up but probably got from someone else, and after a beat of incomprehension it's always met with a slight laugh. *D.I.,* as I call it, is different than an open relationship, because it only happens when one or the other partner is off travelling or at a conference or otherwise out of a city.

My questions are usually meant to be straightforward.

Your reply: "Well. Kind of."

"Kind of? What does that mean?! You've either got it or you don't." I try to sound jovial to seem as if I'm gently prodding rather than needling you.

You look thoughtful but unperturbed, and change the subject.

Our meetings that week are not worth reporting on. We see each other between sessions, ask how our presentations went, and manage a few times to have meals together.

I am fascinated by the layer of hair on your forearms, surprisingly dark, and a dusting of it on your calves (again, revealed below your knee-length shorts). Even with this evidence of hair, I'm thinking that you are quite smooth, perhaps a thin line between your groin and belly, or a patch between your pectoral muscles, reeds peeking up from soil after winter.

I like a smooth body the best, I have to admit, the hand or tongue travelling unobstructed over hard surfaces. Clean like the skin of beluga whales or dolphins or even a pillowcase, my head pressed into it, the weight of a lover on my back, a pulsing, grinding rhythm.

I have brushed up against your body at times, and think your torso is smooth. I know that your body is strong, and the gym weights have left the right kind of evidence that I, a faux-detective, must examine closely.

Thank goodness the tension breaks regularly. When you speak, I'm jarred into a lesser fantasy. In my travels, I've managed to de-eroticize the Canadian accent. Its round open and earnest softness does little to make me hard. Its musical lilts are too familiar. They're like someone in indecision or maybe like elevator music, not the swinging joke of a Glaswegian brogue or the low xylophone tones of a Caribbean parlance. It's friendly and comforting and calms me. It reminds me of friends but does not excite me. I'm glad that there's something in you that I find lacking.

Still, you don't need to talk during sex.

I'm happy to discover that you like foreplay as well. And after-play too, but we can get to that later. Some guys come in about as quick a time as I'm *thinking* of warming up. It's not that I'm a slow starter. It's that I like the tension to build. So, no clothes ripped off, zippers and snaps burning your skin in their rush to flee you. This is about restraint: martini glasses filled with white chocolate mousse, and no one is around anywhere. You could dip your finger in and smooth over the indentation. Would anyone notice? *Hold it in, hold it in, don't spoil your supper.*

My mouth is watering as if I'm already swallowing you and I'm soiling your clothes with saliva, stains of wet at your nipple (if you were a woman, you could be lactating), at your crotch (like a teenager that fantasized too much, too quickly), at the hemline of your shorts (as if you were wading in the ocean). The small of your knee is wet; it echoes your salivating mouth.

Articles of clothing get taken off one at a time, and generally we take turns. I remove your shoe. Then another shoe. You remove my shirt. The process is interrupted because you cannot believe the size of my nipples, and have to check with your tongue to know if they are really that large and round. You suck on them and a space just behind my temples starts to be drawn into the same suction. I unbutton your shorts. And then the buttons at your groin. We do not allow the other to undress himself. Certain procedures must be followed.

Finally, both of us naked, it is like being born again. If we stopped to think about it. Which we do not do since we're occupied with each other's senses and movements, textures beneath our hands. You suck cock as well as you write, and I try to show you my talents too. I put my tongue up your ass, milky white, hard and soft, a marble Italian statue come to life and writhing above my mouth. I have a weakness for strength, and you have it. There are so many muscles in your back, thighs, and shoulders. They shift constantly under my hands, as if I am the wooden bridge to Noah's Ark and all manner of beasts—light, heavy, round, horned—are shifting over my walkway. While my mind tries to take in these various sensations, you add to the difficulty and press into me with human hands, tongue, arms, breath, cock.

I have always fantasized about getting good at being fucked. So why not with you? There was something political about my objections in my early sexual career. Both the "passive Asian" stereotype and being younger and smaller than some of my partners was no excuse, I thought, for me to be the one penetrated.

The various techniques of coercion also left me feeling cold. "Oh, you'll *really* like it"; "It's easy, you just have to relax"; "I bet you've been waiting for it"; "You'll get used to it." I did try with other lovers whom I felt more comfortable with. I mean, I really tried. Endless foreplay. Rimmed like I was a Chevy going through an automatic carwash. Fingers up me like a Dutch dam in need of constant repair. But the moment of truth, when it came, the first time, and most of the next times: *Ow! Ow! Ow!*

One lover told me, "It hurt a lot at first, but when I got used to it, it became my favorite position. I can't get enough of it. I sometimes can't come if I'm not being fucked."

Hmm, this sounded good. "And how long did it take to get used to it?"

"Well, it kind of hurt for the first two years, and then it was OK."

Two years!?

Of course, other friends had no problems at all. "I've been putting things up there as long as I can remember. Candles. Carrots. Lots of *C* things. It's never hurt at all. Maybe try it on your side." "Practise with a dildo," recommended another, who was giving advice from personal experience. The most helpful advice was from my gay doctor, who had asked for a general sexual history in order to figure out my risks for various infections. *Do you get fucked?* I liked that he used the slang rather than a more clinical word like *penetrated.*

"Not really," I said. "I find that it kind of hurts."

Later, his finger up my ass, checking for warts, lesions, and whatever, he commanded, "Squeeze." He inserted his finger further and repeated his command. "You need to ask your lover to do this so that your sphincter muscle is exhausted and gets completely relaxed. If you do this, it should be fine." Businesslike, he removed his glove and turned away. I have no doubt that he was giving no more than helpful professional advice with a useful demonstration.

Since then, I've been fucked on various occasions, sometimes painful, sometimes pleasurable, but always with a little discomfort and never for very long. What would it be like to be as capable as one of those famed bottoms in porno movies, leaning over (or standing up, or on his back, or on his head, or basically any which way) saying "Give it to me"?

So. Give it to me. We haven't discussed this either. But I want this. I'm gagging for it. My anus is puckering like a kiss, and I'm thinking that you're the one. This is it. You inside of me, and me feeling better than I've ever felt before.

Poppers give me a headache, and god, they smell bad but they *work*. Dizzy. Heart beating faster. Sometimes a headache the next day. To avoid that, I take an empty small brown bottle and run it over your skin, capturing your sweat and spit in it, the remains of your day, until I have my own personalized vapor. There's cologne in there too, musky and sweet. I think it's going to have a Japanese name, but you say, no, it's something that's hard to get. But I've got it now, and as I close one nostril with my finger, put the bottle to the other and inhale deeply, there's a chemical effect that burns my skin. My head is pounding. I want you in, in, in.

Your cock is long, not particularly thick, beautifully proportioned and slick with moisture. We smother it in the finest oils and grab a condom, one of the new-technology ones that don't need water-based lube. It makes a strange crinkly sound, but that's OK, it's so thin that it's like a layer of skin, like a spray of water that you use to revive yourself from exhaustion. Your cock glows. From what, I don't know. Heat? Light? My desire? No matter. Fuck me: with all your might.

You knock at my door. When you enter, there is a moment of sharp pain, sweet rather than sour. It is replaced immediately by a pleasure that storms my senses and suddenly my sphincter is exhausted and relaxed, so relaxed that it is lying back at the poolside with a tropical cocktail. With a tiny floral-patterned paper umbrella in it. Served by a Norwegian waiter named Olav. Who is naked. The hair on his arms lit up in the sun like a cornfield. Cheekbones like curved fists. A dick of wonder. The drink makes me giddy and I spill it and laugh and laugh.

You take me through rhythms all night long, a dance party where you lose track of time, the DJ slows and speeds the music, sometimes there are voices, a chorus, sometimes only beats and then this big diva voice brings you up and over and spinning around the room. Sometimes you press into me gently like leaning into the wind, and sometimes you are pounding me like an animal, like television violence. I can feel you up to my stomach, shivering through my legs, to the top of my cock and all through the center of my body. My insides pulse and expand and contract as you slide in and out of me.

We've come to the point of orgasm repeatedly, and pulled ourselves back with deep breaths, tugs on the scrotum, and sudden changes of pace. But now, they are rumbling up like premonitions, like the nerves of animals before a thunderstorm, or the iron figures of lions in China that wait for centuries and finally, when an earthquake is approaching, metal balls hidden in the animals' skulls are jarred loose and fall into their mouths. You see them, their mouths full and you know the moment has arrived.

Though our eyes have closed and opened, our vision sometimes clouded, now, we look at each other clearly. My cock bobs and sways like a conductor's baton. Your hips are tired. Exhaustion ripples through the xylophone bars of your stomach, and up through the striations in your chest. My cum shoots into your chest, wet syllables of laughter, and yours into the condom inside of me. We ejaculate at the moment that dawn breaks.

Whatever happened to liquid paper? I remember a tiny bottle with a black-and-white label. If you left the cap off too long, or the product was too old, it would brush onto the page in a thick paste, unsuitable for writing over.

A classmate, Al Kershaw, who had a fascination for Nazi Germany and the gym (a frightening combination, I thought), shocked all of us by painting swastikas on his tongue and sticking it out at us. Those were the days.

Now, writing takes such different forms. The paper moves onto a screen, ink from pens moves to printer cartridges. We still have use for paper, erasers, carbon paper, liquid paper, and foolscap, but not as often. For me at least, and millions more, there are constant revisions and when we print out a clean copy, you cannot tell what has gone on beforehand.

This is good-bye: the conference is over. We both have late flights. The night before, you came out dancing with friends. We flirted with each other, and I knew that you had some attraction for me. You wore a short sleeve shirt and left the buttons undone. Your torso appeared through that curtain and the definition and contours were more beautiful than I had expected.

Music, celebration, good-byes. Friends and colleagues all around. A distracting atmosphere. When I looked for you next, you had disappeared, and then emerged much later, a Brazilian man with you who hung back at the last minute.

I'm struck again at how handsome your eyes are.

I expect to leave you at the nightclub with your new friend, but when we're about to leave, you ask if you can get a ride with me and my friends. We leave you at your hotel and arrange to meet the next evening for dinner.

The week has reminded me most of high school sexual tension, and I'm giddy with it. Sex is easy as water these days; the fact that this has not been easy makes it all the more exciting. Complicated teenage years where thoughts and worries and words got in the way of anything physical that might have happened. I was not an early bloomer.

Rather than using my newfound confidence to ask *My place or yours?* instead I search for signals in our conversation, shared glances, and body language.

When I knock on your hotel room door, you are in the middle of a phone conversation and ask me to meet downstairs in the bar. Over a cheap gin and tonic, I plot the night out. I could survive if nothing happens. I have much desire but no expectation. But I'd much rather have something happen. I figure dinner, get a bit sloppy over drinks, and then back to your hotel room for hanky-panky.

This is the conversation you recount:

He had asked what you'd been up to. You'd told him about the conference and about dancing last night. He'd asked if you'd met anyone and you'd told him about the

Brazilian. But nothing happened, you explained. You had only kissed him in the corner, a short giddy drunken kiss, and that was all. Boys will be boys.

"And what are you doing tonight?" he demanded.

"Dinner with a friend." Your tone sheepish in response to his jealousy.

"And the friend's name is?"

"Joseph."

"And are you going to have sex with Joseph tonight too?"

I look at him but he doesn't quite look at me, I'm trying to catch his eyes for some response but it's as if I'm looking through a camera viewfinder and I can't get the framing right. There's something in the way: a camera strap, my finger, a tree.

Like you, I know it's not going to happen. Even if you didn't have sex with Mr. Sao Paolo and even if you "kind of" have an open relationship, there is no way that you, or I, can escape the direct question that your boyfriend has asked.

We find a restaurant around the corner, Indian food. It has elegant white tablecloths and glassware, but is too open and bright to be intimate. Still, I spill my confessions.

"Well, and yes, I would, in another circumstance, certainly want to." You can't quite get the words out right. I'm not convinced that you would throw yourself at me at another time, but I think if you were boyfriendless and I threw myself at you, you'd take me up on it.

We talk about the week, and about work, and have a long conversation on writing. You'd like to take some time off. You wonder if you could make it as a writer by giving yourself time to do it. I, on the other hand, never imagine supporting myself through mere words. I write when I can, and have somehow managed to have more success at it than you.

I can't resist dessert, and order *gulab jamon*. You pass on it, though you taste mine. "Too sweet." But the rosewater syrup trickles down my throat and the two round balls (of what substance I've never known) are too much of an obvious metaphor.

"You're not, after a week of sexual tension and mixed messages, going to leave me without anything, after I've jerked off all week thinking about you."

"So it is sexual!"

Of course it's sexual. As well as emotional, intellectual, psychological, historical and spiritual. Literary most of all, but yes, of course, it's sexual. Did I make it sound otherwise, imply that I was after a passionate sexless extramarital encounter abroad with a man I'd eroticized for seven years?

"I want to say good-bye to you in your room. The two of us. I won't try anything."

I do, of course. I turn off the lights, and an oddly weak street lamp pushes bits of white light into the room. My heartbeat quickened, I face you, and you are leaning against the wall. I pull you towards me in an embrace, chaste to start with, like a friend or a brother, my arms sinking around your shoulders, and *V*-shaped back, the contact between us is at the top of our shoulders. The fingers of my right hand reach up to stroke your bald head. Then I relax, breathe deeply and let our torsos press against each other. We hold each other in the most chaste and the most sexual hug as possible, the words of your boyfriend ringing in our ears. A long time passes. This is as much as I'll get.

Suddenly, I press my lips to yours. Our tongues begin to

dance. You taste as good as expected, better, the Indian meal is a memory but the rosewater trickles in at the edges of our mouths. I rip your T-shirt upwards and lean down, my lips, mouth and teeth sinking into your chest, your perfect chest, the edge of a round cumulus cloud, a freshly printed topographical map to explore. Your torso is unmarred; not a single hair breaks its surface. Your left nipple is small and round, the tip of it hard.

"Joseph." You, slightly breathless. "Joseph."

I put each of my hands to your biceps and press myself up.

"I'm sorry," I say.

A tenderness in your gaze.

But I'm not.

I should probably end here. I mean, why *denoue* when I could just leave it at that, pre-cum staining my underpants and I suspect yours as well.

I'd love to make love to you one day. From the way you write about sex, I think you'd be quite hot. The foreplay has certainly been amazing and I can thank you for a number of particularly hot nights stroking myself while stroking you. And there are, after all, the stories we could write after we've done it. First drafts, revisions and final or not-so-final copies. I'll eat your words until I come.

It's not like this narrative demands a particular order—I've lost it anyway, and worst of all have completely stopped pretending that I write about people other than myself.

Of course it's me. My desire on the page.

I learned the word *sublimation* at an early age.

.....

Mistakes Were Made

Richard B.

"Hi Bruce."

"No, I'm not Bruce."

"Oh, well, I'm sure we've met."

"Maybe, I don't think so."

"But you look really familiar."

"Um, sorry..."

.....

Richard B. thinks this is an unusual pickup but yeah, he's kind of hot. Acts too familiar though, never seen this guy before in my life, where do they hide them? "Yeah, I was, born here, high school in North Vancouver. Yeah, I do. She's older than me by about five years. Just got married six months ago."

.....

Richard C.

Where have I seen this guy before? I know I've seen this guy before. I'd like to sleep with him. Have I slept with him before? If I haven't met him then...oh, it's a photo. Oh no, I think it's...

.....

Think, think. It's a school night, the boss is going to want me to finish the Turner job. Can I get him home? Could I get him to leave? Does he look like the kind that would stay the night? I think I'd like that. But then maybe I'd get to work late, and the boss will be mad again, but if I give him my number, will he call...?

.....

Mistakes Were Made

.....

Oh god, he knows my sister.

Oh god, I dated his sister.

.....

They agree to go to Richard C.'s. It's closer and Richard C. has an earlier start in the morning. On the way out, they meet someone who knows Richard C. Or maybe not, doesn't stop and chat. Acts kind of funny. Hmm, what was that about?

Hmm. Glad he agreed to come back to mine. Let's go. Oh yuck, psycho-ex Calvin. I'll have to introduce him. Damn, what is his name again...*R*, it starts with *R*. Ralph. Robert. Ronan. Oh yeah, same as mine. "Oh hi Calvin, this is..." Harrumph. Walked right by. Well I never.

.....

Oh, damn, thinks Richard B. I forgot my contact lens cases. They'll be glued to my eyes in the morning. I won't be able to see a thing.

Oh, damn, thinks Richard C. Where are my keys. Checks front pockets, back pockets. Argh. Backpack. Oh, there. The tiny pocket.

.....

"Keep your voice down, my flatmate's asleep and the walls are a bit thin."
"Really?" says Richard B., in full voice. "What did you say again you did for a living?"

I hope Martin's taken his sleeping tablets tonight, he thinks. Remembers that Martin pretends to get angry at the noise, but is angry that someone else is getting laid, and it's not him.

.....

They play around. Richard B. looks around at the bedroom. Cluttered, as if Richard C. is

Oh god, he can tell by the ceramic on wood sound that it's broken, irreparable, a gift

.....

still a university student. They're tongue-kissing, a bit of a battle really, each is trying to shove his own tongue in the other's mouth as far as it can go. Unexpectedly, Richard C. turns out to in and sucks hard. "Ow, ow!" Richard B. would say but can't speak. But he's turned on, leaps forward pushing Richard C. back onto the mattress, his left leg flies up and knocks over the bedside lamp, with a great ca-chunk.

.....

Maybe this is a mistake. Richard B. surveys the scene: Richard C. is contorting wildly, stretching, grimacing. "Cramp..." he moans. Rhymes with camp, thinks Richard B. "I think I'm OK now." Meek grin.

Thank god, let's get on with it.

.....

from his parents and his mother always looks for it when she comes over. What is she going to say? Still, Richard C. is turned on and falls back willingly onto the mattress, lets his arms and legs be manipulated up and down, bent at the joints. The dial of his heartbeat notches up incrementally, and he's starting to feel in rhythm, Richard B. sprawled over him, his left leg straight out, and right bent back. "Oh oh oh... Get off, charley horse."

.....

Richard C. finds Richard B.'s pleasure spot, and it's his nipples, no doubt about it. He pinches, licks, bites, and presses down into them with fingers and tongue. Richard C. is suddenly alarmed. It's like a swarm of bees arriving. "What is that? What's happening?" But it's unstoppable, this moan modulating up and down and in rhythm like a police siren.

.....

Mistakes Were Made

.....

All of a sudden, Richard B.'s head jerks up. Richard B. lives alone and is not used to sounds in his apartment. "What's that?" he breaks out of his moaning and his voice is surprisingly pedestrian. The wall thumps. Three loud knocks.

"Oh no," thinks Richard C., "a moaner...." Rolling his eyes at the knocking sound, and looking up at Richard B., whose eyes had been shut in ecstasy, his head tilted up into a pillow, but now is jumpy, eyes open like a scared rabbit.

.....

Thump thump.
A flatmate? Jeezus.
I was enjoying that.
And now he looks a bit pissed off.

"Look, we've woken up my flatmate, can you be a bit more quiet?" Thinks: And I haven't even gotten his pants off yet.
So he does. Grabs pants and underwear in one grip and yanks both down.
Richard B.'s cock is large, and bends slightly to heaven rather than hell.

.....

Did I really hear that?
If Richard B. wasn't enjoying this blow job so much, he'd think of a retort, or something vengeful.
Mmmmm. Mmmmm.

Are you sure you're Chinese?" says Richard C., not thinking.
Goes down.
Ahruwgggllgglll...

.....

Oh god, I hope he's a bottom.

Oh god, I hope he's a bottom.

.....

"So, um. Do you have a favorite way of coming?"

Man, he talks a lot. "I've got lots of ways I like coming."

.....

.....

Uh huh, turn the question back, I wish people were just more honest.

"Well, I'm basically...a top."

.....

Richard B. turns on him. "So, you think just because I'm Asian that I'll make a better bottom." He lacks humor when he says this. Ha ha. Got him back. *Please please please.*

.....

He crouches down and examines the contents under the sink. Interesting. Unpleasant. Soap. Shoe polish (?). Deodorant. Rusty razor blades. The lube is prominently out in front on the bottom shelf, left side, three varieties. *Slik*. *Wet*. And one with a black label with orange lettering. What does it say? *Deep Heat*. Must be new. He grabs Slik instead, upturns the bottle to test it

Fixes him with a killer stare. "What about you?"

.....

Please please please.

"Oh. Uh. Me too."

.....

Richard C. feels guilty and consents. "But you'll have to go easy on me. I think I'll need some poppers, I'll have to get them from the freezer, will you grab some lube from the shelves under the sink in the loo?"

.....

Damn, damn, where is it? Richard C. is wondering if Martin, who is neater than Richard, has done something with his amyl. He scans the top shelf, then the bottom, checks in the side door. No, no no. He shifts around freezer-burnt leftovers, packets of frozen steak and minced beef. Knocks the ice cube tray on its side. Finally finds his small bottle under the frozen peas.

• • • • •

out, and Slik comes pouring out after the unscrewed lid. Agh. Stands up to look for a cloth. Oh. Ah. Ouch, Richard B. slips on the lube on the shiny floor. Lands hard on his ass. Oh, the fuck with it. He grabs all three bottles.

• • • • •

Richard B.'s rushed back into the room, he's rubbing his ass and hopes it doesn't bruise, plans to look relaxed, but why is he taking so long? Glances up, there's a Post-it note on the mirror. Says *Didn't want to wake you up. You looked too sweet. Have fun tonight at ARQ. Love, Ed.*

• • • • •

Oh, what a slag. I wonder if he takes someone home every night of the week.

• • • • •

Now it takes him a while to get back in the mood. He's hard but not hard enough.

Hope this hasn't gone stale. He pauses, thinks how tired he's going to be at work tomorrow, wonders if he can finish the Turner job. Thinks how sexy Richard B. is. God, he's even got dimples when he smiles. Yes!

• • • • •

Richard C. comes rushing in with the poppers. He's a bit nervous, sometimes he just can't relax enough so that it doesn't hurt. And it does hurt, still. Why do all the porn stars make it look so easy? He looks at Richard B. and notices a funny expression on his face. It's a glimmer of something, and Richard C. is good at picking up small cues. He looks at him, and out of the corner of his eye sees the Post-it note on the mirror. Oh, I knew I should have taken that down! I hope he doesn't think...

• • • • •

"Sorry, sorry..." They're midway into passion, and Richard C. lifts off of Richard B.'s finally

Especially for a tight asshole. They kiss, he feels hotter and hornier. He's ready, it's working, it's...

.....

What the hell. Even with the delays, Richard B. is very pleased at being a top. It's fantastic really. He loves a good fuck. He's envisioning it happening before it happens, lies on his back practising slow thrusting upward motions with his groin. Come on baby, get out of the bathroom, come to Richard, I'm ready for you, I'll teach you how to be fucked. His arms restless, hands grabbing the sheet below him, he makes a sudden motion, which knocks over the half open bottle of poppers.

.....

All of these mishaps remind Richard B. of when he was travelling in Europe, Poland of all places. He was staying in a cheap hotel with other young travellers. He'd been nervous, he wasn't a confi-

hard cock. "I've got to piss. It's all the pressure on my prostate. I'll just be a sec."

.....

"What have you done?" Richard B has his butt up in the air like a French maid pawing at the mattress, with a dazed look at his face. "Not with my shirt. That's my Paul Smith vest. Stop, stop..." The room will smell of this for months and no amount of air freshener will get rid of the haze of amyl. Richard C. will become slower at work, dream of fast heartbeats and group sex. When Richard B. sleeps over, he'll dream of wet steam and rocking horses.

.....

All of these mishaps remind Richard C. of going home with a guy who lived in a cheap student home with one straight guy, a lesbian couple, a man of undetermined sexuality, two cats and one dog.

dent traveler, but the look on this tough, punky young thing was obvious, and too compelling to resist. Especially when Alex, who didn't seem to speak a word of English, thrust his door number into his hand that afternoon, and looked up at him with puppy-dog eyes. That night, after a tiring day of sightseeing, he'd knocked at the door. Even then, they hadn't rushed into each other's arms, had been slow and tentative, shedding their clothes, Richard starting to unwind. Settled onto the bed, Richard wasn't at all sure about Alex's nipple rings, and the crude tattoo on his chest, you couldn't see these with his clothes on. But he picked up rhythm, and soon, they were dry humping on the narrow bed, which not two minutes later collapsed, the middle falling through onto the floor, the mattress tilted towards the base. They looked at each other with wide eyes

The door to Shane's small bedroom was off the hinges. They fell into a heap of passion on his bed, started stripping off clothes, heard voices and stopped. Shane leaned the door up against the frame, an imperfect fit, but it provided them with some modicum of privacy. The floorboards were long and uneven, and the vibrations of the bed on the floor had no small effect. Shane was on his back with Richard on top of him, when Richard saw Shane's eyes widen and his mouth start to form a shout. The door was falling in slow motion directly onto Richard's back. It fell with a thud. No bruising or major injury but it was difficult to get off, and Shane was mortally embarrassed. Not helped by Jenine and Penny rushing over to see what the fuss was about, seeing the two naked men struggling to get the door off of them, and pealing with uncontrollable laugh-

• • • • •

and examined the bed, finding the mattress held up with only thin slats of wood resting across the box frame. Neither of them could continue.

• • • • •

Being with a beginner is good and bad. Bad because of the wait, and the awkwardness, and what if it doesn't happen anyway? Good because it's exciting, and you feel like an explorer planting a flag on new ground. Richard B. reaches for the lube.

• • • • •

Ah... Oh, oh oh. MmmmMmmm. Hmm... Ah ah ah. Arrooohhh. Uhhhhh.

• • • • •

Hmm. Interesting sounds, thinks Richard B., and suddenly remembers his first lover, who laughed after he came, so full of joy was he. Sweet. Richard takes a deep breath, smiles helplessly and carefully unrolls the condom

ter that continued as Shane apologized and Richard dressed, suggesting they make a date for another time.

• • • • •

"Lube!" he calls out. He's not used to this. Luckily there were more poppers in the freezer, though there's a high chance that Martin is going to get pissed off that he's borrowed them. He grabs the bottle, inhales deeply. This time, he screws the lid back on tightly. His body relaxes.

• • • • •

Ah.... Nnngghh, nnngghh. Oo oo oo. Arrr, arrr, ohoooo. Eeeeeee.

• • • • •

Hmm. Interesting sounds, thinks Richard C., and somehow remembers a sauna incident when the person he was with said, "Merry Christmas" after he came. Odd. Richard stretches his back, feels his pulse slow down again, looks from his cock. Ah, success.

• • • • •

"So how was it?"

"Um. Good."

"Like good, but not fantastic, like you endured it rather than enjoyed it?"

"No, it felt pretty good."

Richard B. looks at Richard C., a hint of concern, a hint of affection.

• • • • •

They lie back in postcoital bliss, and Richard B. snores ever so lightly, a tiny flutter of a sound. When he wakes up, he's horny again. He wakes up Richard C. with kisses, and suddenly they're at it again. A quick jerk-off, he figures, and they'll fall back to sleep. Oh god, I love that; Richard C.'s tongue is in his ear, surrounded by hot breath, fresh out of sleep. He reaches over and grabs another bottle of lube.

• • • • •

Ow, ow, ow! What the fuck's

thoughtful but happy. Mmm, success.

• • • • •

"And you? How was it with an amateur?"

"Wonderful." He sounds sincere.

"Well," says Richard C., "I've never come with someone inside me before." Then immediately regrets saying it. Oops. Honesty. On a first date. Said too much.

• • • • •

They lie back in postcoital bliss, and Richard C. dozes off to the steady sound of Richard B.'s heavy, slightly congested breaths. He's awoken by lips upon him, soft and hard. I love to be woken up by sex, he thinks, throwing himself into their somnambulant dance. They're kneeling on the bed, hands exploring each other; Richard B. reaches down with a handful of lube, covers their cocks in the greasy liquid. The hot liquid. The... Oww!

• • • • •

Richard C. gingerly soaps

• • • • •

happening, Richard B. is tumbling over Richard C. as they're both trying to get off the bed, then running naked into the hallway as they're hollering and into the shower which is too hot then too cold...

• • • • •

"Oh hi." A bleary-eyed stranger looks at them through the open door of the bathroom. "Uh, sorry, little problem with the, what's it called, Deep Heat." Normally Richard B. would feel embarrassed: a total stranger looking at him naked, but what can he do?

• • • • •

They eventually manage to fall asleep again, but not before more cuddling, and a range of amusement from a sheepish grin, to belly laughing. Rather than hearing banging from Martin's room next door, when they laugh too loudly, they hear him laughing as well. He dreams with the sound of it in his ears.

• • • • •

them down, tries to get the water to the right temperature, sees skin turning red, burning and tingling. He suddenly realizes what happened. "You grabbed the Deep Heat, didn't you? It's for sprains..."

• • • • •

Richard C. sees his flatmate Martin's sour face breaking into convulsive laughter. His wide eyes fixed on their red thighs and groins. His back, still shaking with giggles as he returns to his room. At least he won't be angry now at the noise they've made.

• • • • •

Richard C. doesn't think he's ever quite had a night like this, he can imagine them telling people this anecdote, he can imagine them together. They sleep deeply, and in the morning, Richard C. can't bear to wake Richard B. He sets the alarm for half an hour later, writes a note, and leaves him in his bed.

• • • • •

Mistakes Were Made

.....

Richard B. hears the alarm, and amazingly figures out how to shut it off. He smells of sex, even he can tell. That, and Deep Heat, and the calamine lotion, which was the only thing Richard C. could find to try to soften the pain.

He makes two faces. Yuck. Mmmm. He examines himself in the mirrored door to the wardrobe and is suddenly curious. He rifles through shirts, underwear, shoes. Finds a shirt he dislikes and hides it behind another but hmm, Richard C.'s taste is not so bad. He could actually wear almost everything, shirts, pants, shoes, maybe the suit would be a bit big in the shoulders.

He throws on a shirt, for fun. Within the month, their wardrobes will be completely intermingled.

Soon, they'll be indistinguishable.

Richard C. makes it to work on time, is amazingly productive in the morning, even if his groin is still itchy. How did the lube get mistaken for Deep Heat? He arranges to meet his best friend for lunch to tell him all about it.

"Oh, that's unforgivable," says catty Andrew.

"What, what?" says Richard C. Sometimes he thinks Andrew is hilarious. Sometimes he thinks Andrew tries too hard to be funny.

"Homo-sexxxxual relationships I can handle," each syllable punctuated like the keys of a manual typewriter. "Homo-professional relationships are disturbing. I mean, two lawyers in the same house... But darling, the same name! Homo-nominal relationships!" He turns his head back and forth three times. "No, no, no. It's not *allowed* to last...."

.....

If It Sticks Out

If it sticks out: look at it. Is it small as a pearl, glistening and taking in the world around it onto its lustrous surface? Or big as a leg of lamb, roasted, the fat and juices still sizzling and dripping, delicious and pink? Somewhere in between? Examine your own body. Can it fit somewhere? One, two, maybe three places. How does it lean? Does it point towards the sun or the moon, inland or the coast, the sky, or hidden places below?

Is it round? Circle it. Mirror it with your eyes, your pupils the same shape. Trace its aureole. Cup it with your hand. Put your ear against it. Bounce off of it. Rebound onto it. Kiss it, closed-mouth. Close your eyes. Draw it from memory.

If it sticks out, lick it. Orbit it with your tongue, clockwise, counter-clockwise. Ten times. Inhale, and let the breath dry the saliva on your tongue. Extend that tongue, curl it towards gravity, approach the object, roll your head into it like a cat, like a golfer's swing, slow motion. Withdraw your tongue into your mouth and taste it. Rub it against your upper palate, close your eyes and see the shelf where all the tastes in the world are stored. Is it there, this ruby you've gathered up between your lips? If it is, point it out, nod, pay it respect. If it's new, place it in a glass case of your favorite color. Make space for it on the shelf.

If it sticks out, cover it. Form spit on your tongue, get the saliva flowing from your gums and cheeks, part your lips gently, just the front, as if about to whistle. Position yourself over it and let fall one shining drop. Listen to the sound it makes. Continue until it's slick with spittle, until the dry roof has been covered in autumn rain. Is it shining? Blow on it. Steadily and then in sharp hot breaths. Give it a wolf whistle.

If it sticks out, it's a monument, it's a tourist attraction. Look up, and see it above you. The lights at night falling over you like the start of rain. Now, climb its stairs. You can take the elevator but you'll have to pay. Enjoy the view.

If it sticks out, engulf it, seal up the borders. You're China; it's Hong Kong pre-'97. You surround it but it belongs to someone else. Be glad you don't own it. Treasure it like a gift from a foreign land that you'd never seen or heard of before.

Is it beautiful? Do you find it beautiful? Wrap it in leather straps, no, bind it. Tight so the skin pushes out from beneath, and the blood is near the surface, so if you place your fingernail against it, the indentation stays and is surrounded by a cloud of white. If it is the longest or the shortest day of the year, or any spirit day that you wish to celebrate, use the straps laced with shiny studs, bind it twice. Adorn it in your finest jewelry, gold studs and silver bars. Pierce it. Show it no fear.

If it sticks out, suck it. Like your life depended on it. This is the soother you've been waiting for. Pull it in, feel it slide past your lips. Introduce it to the darkness inside your mouth. Compare the shape of it with your tongue's shape.

Andy Quan

.....

Comfort it with the silk of your palate and the insides of your cheeks, soft and clean. Like submerging in a freshwater lake some black summer night, a lightning storm in the distance. Suck harder. Feel it at the back of your throat, like a premonition. Jostling with your uvula. This cavity that's been bothering you lately—it's filled and the pain is gone.

If it sticks out, paint it. You've got a palette with colors that have no names in this language. Oils and powders made from bumblebees' legs, seahorses' gullets, the wings of a hummingbird, distilled sapphires, the plume of a south China dragon. Here's your blank canvas, its cells and pores open up to you. Paint something from a part of your mind you haven't visited lately. Spell out the word, *desire*. Sketch in an outline at first, or not at all, go free-form, slather it on, you can always thin it out, or paint over it. Remember the hottest you've ever felt, and make a picture of it. Or the fleshiest. Or wettest. Connect the dots. Color over the lines. Remember the loudest sound you've ever heard. Remember the time you almost went blind. Go on. Use your imagination.

If it sticks out, sit on it. Have a seat and swing your legs like you're sitting on a tiny outcrop above the Grand Canyon. Half the world's wonder is there, and a whole mountain could fit in, or the Black Forest, or the lake that you grew up beside. Feel it beneath you, on your backside, the object that is preventing you from falling. Falling into all of that.

Now, sit on it like you're in a schoolyard playground. First, the seesaw. The stained red-orange wood has captured an afternoon's sun, it's warm on your buttocks, your bare thighs stick to it. Push down with your legs, and you're up, suspended. To get down, think weight. Breathe in heavy air, lower your shoulders, relax until your torso has taken on new density. Unsuccessful? Ask then. Request that your partner let you down, you'll know the best tone of voice: polite, playful, commanding. Strike a deal? Say it's your turn.

Now, we're on the swings. You grip the chains so hard the blood runs out of your fingers. Start slowly and the wind against your face is like you're being painted with brushes made of squirrels and pussy willows. Then you pump your legs in front of you faster and faster: you're exhilarated and soothed at the same time. Your stomach catches with fear and pleasure as you kick your legs out, the arc getting wider and wider. You fly up face forward into the sky before you're taken backwards again, a rhythmic rocking: one, two, three, four. If you choose to jump off, midair, you will learn flight, excitedly clawing and scraping at the air. There's soft sand below you, and children can fall without breaking bones.

. . . . .

Rufo

One recipe for disaster, or at least for a very bad meal, is to desperately need or want some critical element and not have it at hand. Does one forge ahead anyway? Is it mind over matter? Is there room for substitution or experimentation?

The beginning had the makings of a fine romance. I was living in Brussels, home of a strange small statue of a pissing boy of inordinate fame, the world's best chocolatiers, and a growing infrastructure for the new Eurocracy: the European Union and Parliament expanding by the year along with its army of sharply-suited professionals and multilingual interpreters. I'd arrived, having proudly told friends I'd hit the quarter-century mark, to work in the office of a small human rights organization; so small, in fact, that I was the only employee.

My office was at the top of an empty four-floor seventeenth-century building. From the outside, a New Worlder like me was struck with a sense of cool wonder at the ancient grey stones holding together through time. From the inside, one simply wondered how the building held together at all. I'd struggled with the catches of the enormous tall, thin windows for the whole winter, trying to combat the stuffy, dank air while simultaneously fending off the cold. The stairs creaked, lightbulbs blew and it amazed me that I could keep my laptop computer powered. Its hum was my only company during those months since the building was completely empty during the day—a small bar opened on the ground floor in the evening, and the first floor was occasionally used for meetings of similarly tiny left-leaning groups.

Rufo arrived one afternoon as the season turned to spring.

"I'm interested in volunteering," he offered by way of introduction. "I've done a Masters Degree in international law."

His hair was short and blond, an elegant black shirt covered his husky frame and his wide blue eyes looked so lively I thought he might break into a folk dance. I offered him a seat across from me. Soon, he had casually stretched his leg out and through the desk so that it touched mine.

"I wasn't really interested in volunteering," he admitted, sprawled naked on my bed an hour later. "I saw you in the bar and found out where you worked." I had thought that Italians—he was one—were supposed to be dark and swarthy, but that wasn't true in this case. Still, his scent was of soft white bread drizzled in olive oil.

Rufo Felaco. I liked the first name—the last sounded too close to *fellatio*, fine in practice but preferred unsaid. He *seemed* perfect: educated, literate, musical and in good employment. Like the rest of a whole squadron of well-schooled men and women from Western and Northern Europe, he worked at the European Commission, where they were classified according to divisions that worked under Director-Generals. You could overhear their conversations: "Are you in DG 5? I'm in DG 13. He's just transferred to DG

1B from DG 1A." I could never quite figure out what any of them did, and simply referred to them as Eurocrats. In any case, it was a stable job.

He claimed to have at least another degree besides the one in law—something environmental, which sounded both fashionable and altruistic. He'd led a choir at his last workplace (which DG, I didn't know) and I imagined his hands drawing order into the air. In addition to Italian, he spoke English and French fluently, with a smattering of German.

He also had a strong body which brought my senses to rapt attention each time I was in his presence—so much that I'd asked him in the midst of our first love-making whether he was a bodybuilder.

"Oh, come on!" He looked incredulous, which told me right away of both my insecurity and my lack of experience with the male body. Still, I loved his curves: round, buoyant biceps; the soft half-balloon shape of his ample pectoral muscles decorated with precise brown-pink nipples; the slight curve of his long, thick cock. His body had a fullness; I could grab on to parts of it like handles while my tongue fell naturally into grooves and crevices. He was happy to be tasted from head to toe, and would also return the attention. I would take as much of his scrotum into my mouth as fit, sucking gently, then press my lips together gently around his testicles. The sound he made, a rough, guttural moan, I thought of as particular to the Mediterranean, sailors and students alike, masculine and primal, in the markets and on the docks.

Best of all I found over the next weeks that he seemed to like me, and with a focused, romantic passion that endeared him to me. It made me realize that I had worked months for too many hours, meeting too few people.

A few days after our first meeting, we made love again at his apartment. The place in Brussels where I could afford to rent was small and comfortable, in a modern apartment building with an uncanny resemblance to the apartment building where I'd lived in Toronto the year before. Rufo's was in a gorgeous old building with a romantically drafty stairwell. It had been renovated recently and the interiors sparkled but kept the charm of the past: high ceilings and windows, and strangely shaped rooms since the old building had never been intended to be modern apartments.

His mattress was on the floor. Like most Italians, outward appearances were more important to him than what lay hidden in one's apartment. As further evidence, he pointed to a suit jacket hanging on a door handle with a laugh both ashamed and proud. "It's Issey Miyake," he told me. It was of the strangest shape, a length halfway between a jacket and an overcoat, made of an incredibly fine material that hung elegantly down the torso, as if arranged by gravity. "Try it on," he said and held it out to me.

I declined and removed my clothes instead. His wide, thick tongue slid into my mouth and I pressed my tongue against it. We made love in the perfect light of day, the morning sun a welcome third partner. We moved over each other's bodies with care and equality, my physical desire for Rufo suddenly elevated by the absences in the past and the promise of the future. I wanted to be in love and was hungry for more than the meager bits I'd had before. While I had started to become more sexually experienced in the last year or two, the idea of a *boyfriend* or *lover* was new to me.

.....

The shower was out in the hallway; he offered me a robe to traverse it. I still felt flashes of hot lust as he stepped out of his. As we showered together he wiped the dried semen from my belly with a washcloth. "All that wasted life," he sighed in a joking way. The sudden injection of Catholicism brought me out of my reverie with a jolt, reminding me that he had a life that stretched into a past far beyond the last hour, or days.

But we did not delve into that past. Over the next weeks we saw each other every few days for a drink or dinner or sex but didn't really establish any sort of routine. Early on in this period, I met some of his friends, in a far suburb of Brussels, an area I'd never visited. This was another advantage of having a boyfriend, opportunities for something new. We pulled up in his car to a modest apartment; inside were three friends: a fashion designer, an Italian administrator, and her husband, another Italian; I didn't quite catch his profession.

"We'll go sailing," he told them, "in the south of Italy in May." He hadn't told me about this idea beforehand and I was offended. Men may be sloppy at communication, but neither do we take well being told what to do. But I hid my annoyance. It was the first time I'd met any of his friends and I wanted to make a good impression. All of them seemed nice enough, polite with a certain impassivity.

"What do you think of that?" He grinned goofily.

I pictured two scenes. There was the Italy of my imagination, since I had never visited that part of Europe. The sun poured lazily onto a seaside landscape cobbled together from photos, magazines and book covers. However, the second scene was of a small boat in the middle of the ocean, far from shore, possibly circled by sharks (in Italy?) with no escape in sight. Unless you're a gambler, not somewhere you want to get to know someone.

"We've only been together a few weeks," I told him later, at which he looked hurt. We made love again, this time in a distracted and slow tempo. Even our ejaculations seemed to have less force. Rufo looked at our sticky torsos, and slid into his joke-telling voice.

"All that wasted life."

You're repeating yourself, I thought but didn't say aloud.

I carry a weight on my shoulders. I've tried to learn to walk in a way that it doesn't show. I try to bounce off of my heels and look light. I try not to slump. But since my first days of going to gay bars and meeting gay men, I could never tell what their reaction would be to me, and how often it had to do with the color of my skin.

I try not to talk about this because people find it boring or distasteful or they don't really want to hear it. "Why are you guys such whiners?" commented one man I'd barely met, watching a screening of a short documentary on gay Asian Canadians. "I mean, I'm attracted to Asians. I saw this guy walking down the street yesterday and said to myself, 'Wow, he's really handsome in a *white* sort of way.' "

Another time I tried to explain to a friend over dinner, "Don't you think there is something wrong about someone telling me that they're not attracted to me because I'm Asian, rather than saying, 'sorry, I'm not attracted to you'?"

"Yeah, but there are some guys who only go for Asians, those sixty-year-old guys, what about them?"

Yeah. What about them?

Andy Quan

.....

Where would you ever see the statement "no Asians" except in gay personal ads?

So I admit I'm equipped with as many defensive capabilities as James Bond's car. It's both to protect myself from the careless racism I've described and to fend off those who are interested in me *only* because of my race.

I'm usually pretty good at spotting the warning signs. I ask the men I date early on about their ex-boyfriends and I can usually figure out without asking if they were Asian or not. I find out whether they've lived in Asia for periods of time, or travelled there (especially to Thailand), or whether they've developed a special fascination for Eastern Religion.

I'd detected none of these things with Rufo but a week or two after the aborted sailing incident, I ran into an acquaintance at the local bar.

"I saw your picture," said Gung Pei. He said this in an encouraging way, his eyebrows raised on a sharp-featured face. He was from Shanghai and was tall and angular.

I hadn't even known that Rufo had a photo of me.

"Yes, he was showing everyone in the bar."

I might have felt flattered, but felt suspicious instead.

The next time we met, Rufo buried his nose in the corner of my neck, inhaled deeply and looked me in the eyes. "I love the way you smell, did I ever tell you that?"

"I'm not wearing any cologne," I confessed.

"No. It's you. You've got a smell that's like no one else's."

I might have felt flattered, but felt like food instead. *Chinese take-out?*

Still I wasn't sure about him either in a good or a bad way. We carried on a show of interest in each other's lives and he didn't seem to be overly fascinated with me, meaning that I didn't feel like I was being pinned like a butterfly into a collection, my wings studied carefully—the feeling I often got from white men who only were interested in Asians.

Over time though, I found out about more of Rufo's friends: a Vietnamese waiter, an assistant at the Japanese Consul, some of Gung Pei's crowd.

"So, do you know every Asian man in Brussels?" I asked him.

"Well, I try." He laughed and seemed proud rather than what I'd hoped for: embarrassed, sheepish.

I questioned myself. Was it internal racism, some deep-seated dislike for my own kind? No, I decided. I was mystified as to why Rufo would actively seek to be around one race of people.

I once met a man who'd decided that of all wines, he would only drink white, and of that, only chardonnay. While I recognize that there are great variations in a multitude of chardonnays, I can't relate to that narrowing of vision.

I could have tried to ignore this issue but the other parts of Rufo's personality weren't drawing me in either. Try as I might, I couldn't find the person that I expected from the qualifications and talents that I'd mentally latched on to at our first meeting. Now, the conversation clunked rather than sparkled. He listened to me with a fine imitation of interest, but never seemed to remember much of what I said. I may have wanted something to take me away from the loneliness of arriving in a new country, but *this* something wasn't working.

"You and your blond hunks," commented Brent, one of the few of my friends who'd met Rufo. With one fell swoop, he'd reduced all my tastes in men to one stereotype, and reduced Rufo to two words. I was bothered not by how wrong but how right he was.

It continued with no great reason for months. He would be away for business, then I. We'd meet up in between and I would look unhappy, annoyed, distracted, bothered and uninterested. None of these expressions ever seemed to be noticed. None of them ever actually involved telling him what I was feeling. I tried unsuccessfully to think of ways to bring the relationship to a close but I had taught myself too well to avoid confrontation or honesty and neither of us was quite ready for those things, or so I told myself.

In the meantime, he began dropping hints of interest in other men. A Thai waiter. An Asian-American tourist. A beautiful Japanese man in Rome. "I wish he were a prostitute," he said and suddenly a cliché flashed before my eyes as if upon the brightest marquee in London's West End:

What did I ever see in this man?

Had he wanted to hire a sex worker in Italy but just couldn't find one who was Asian?

I also heard of his plans to bring a young Korean man to Brussels for a special program of study in law. He would be staying in Rufo's apartment temporarily.

The last meeting had a poor excuse. He'd borrowed a hard-to-get book, an academic text, heavy and expensive. I wanted it back. With sadness, I suddenly realized that sometimes this is what it comes down to: material objects, how easy or difficult they are to replace.

I decided to combine the task of retrieving the book with another experiment. I knew I was still physically attracted to

Rufo. So what if he wanted his own little Asian boy? I would exoticize him as well. Could I have sex with my fair, muscular Italian, even though I had come to dislike him as a person?

"Hmm... That smells wonderful. Are we eating Chinese tonight?"

"It's Indian curry," I snapped at him, turning off the stove.

We barely finished the meal before stumbling into bed.

I grabbed him roughly, his thick arms and rectangular torso; my teeth went towards his neck, and I pulled at the bottom of his polo shirt so it became free of his jeans. I slid my hand up his shirt, pinched firmly at his chest and nipple, and then pushed him to the bed.

"I want you to fuck me," he said. We hadn't actually fucked before. I was relatively inexperienced sexually and had not discovered anal pleasure. Most of all, I hated the expectation I was usually saddled with as an Asian man: BOTTOM, written across my forehead in big, black brushstrokes and faux-Oriental letters.

As for Rufo, I hadn't known if he liked to be fucked. He'd never offered. I paused for only a second, before saying, "OK. I'll get the condoms and lube." (Another sign of my sexual inactivity, the condoms were in a distant drawer rather than next to my bed.)

But when I returned with them, he said, "Actually, I want to fuck you."

My anger: at his dishonesty, his *sloppy* dishonesty, at my inability to speak, at myself for being so lonely. Instead, I straddled his torso with my knees, quickly came onto his chest, hopped off, and went to take a shower.

All that wasted life.

Andy Quan

.....

"Hey, isn't there any dessert?" he asked as I shoved him out of my apartment and closed the door.

For several years after this I warned friends and coworkers not to give him my new e-mail addresses. But he finally tracked me down. He'd moved to Korea and I to Australia. He wrote: "Did I ever tell you I believe you and me are somehow connected with each other?"

I replied to his e-mail, curtly but politely, and ignored the question.

People talk about boyfriends from hell. But when I look back, I see two ugly boyfriends. Him, ugly in a slightly oafish way, a clueless, fumbling, wide-eyed, took-me-along-for-the-ride-and-never-quite-got-it, insensitive male sort of thing. Those stories you recount about your exes? I'd tell friends, "turned out to be dumb as a rock." I'd ball my right hand into a fist and make a grinding boulder-like motion in the palm of my left.

My real anger, however, is reserved for myself: for expecting too much, hoping for too much, not being able to say what I wanted to—for missing the warning signs and finding myself going out with someone who gave me the creeps and made me feel betrayed. And for being pissed off for so long and still not quite able to take what the world dishes out. For being inexperienced and ugly with insecurity. I'm angry that I'm not someone you'd want to get involved with.

.....

Positive

Your skin is translucent, a thin layer of warm glass like the pane of a picture frame, the painting below of soft whites and pinks with constellations of beauty marks and freckles. The heat passing into me through my hands resting on your back. Perfect conduction of energy.

I never meet men in bars or at dance parties, though I've met hundreds of men who do. Finally, I break my never—at a dance party in Sydney, a yearly fund-raiser for the state AIDS organization. There, chemically flying on ecstasy bumped up with hits of acid, I wandered through the crowd aimlessly, wearing a halo of lights and haze and spare vibrations from the dance track.

Did you see me first? Did I see you? All I know is that I stopped. Then joined in your swaying: unusual movements, your shoulders mostly up around your ears as if your whole body could disappear, melt and be sucked into a hole in the middle of your chest.

"Well, aren't you cute?" Your voice is somehow clear above the music. You touch my arms above the elbows gently. A studded collar around your neck with spikes of fake danger, bare torso, shiny black pants that match your dark pupils. You lean in to kiss me and I fall and fall and fall.

When I come to, we're in another place in the dance hall.

"I'd like to take you home with me." Your voice has laughter in it. That and a melody, a tenor saxophone line in an upper octave, clear and precise, warm as spring coming on.

Nodding is all I do.

"But I want to tell you something first. I'm HIV positive. Have been for ten years, never been sick. I just wanted to make sure you're OK with that. Some people have a problem with it."

Positive, I think. "No problem." My blood is negative. My mind is positive. Yes. Yes. Yes. "Take me home."

We're awake and weary and tired and buzzed up when we fall across your white sheets. "Turn over," you command and your hands are upon me, long and firm strokes of massage up and down the length of my back, shoulders and neck, scalp, and then lower down, buttocks, thighs, calves, feet. "Now, the other side." My nipples hardening under the circles of your palms, my cock lifting up to touch your thighs as you kneel over me.

We're stripped naked. You're not a big man. You have a slim, sculpted muscularity and I would guess a fast metabolism. Also, the texture of an older man, skin moves easily below my fingers above a strength that has taken time to build.

Size is a nice surprise, and I'm astonished. Your cock is enormous. Dark and round and thick. Ecstasy takes away my hunger, but this makes me famished. I want to eat and drink for days at a banquet table fit for the king and queen of all those old countries that still hang on to royalty.

We make love for hours, and move between massage and long kisses and my mouth on your cock and yours on my anus.

I want to do the same to you, but you say, no, it's dangerous.

Neither of us can come with the drugs still coursing through our systems. For what seems like hours, I go through a stage of having to leave the bed every few minutes to urinate. But in the end, side by side, my head on your chest, hands on that astonishing skin, we come to a natural finish.

"It was amazing."

"I wanted to make sure that you felt you could do anything, and that we didn't have to fuck if you didn't want to."

"Well, maybe next time."

You look at me with a glint in your eyes.

Positive. Words repeat in my mind. *Yes. Yes. Yes.*

You become all of the positive lovers I have ever had and will ever have. What is unique to you, I revel in. I eroticize. I turn you into the letters of the word *desire.* I know it is perverse to do this. But is this not who we are, what we are, where our potential lies: the possibility of moving beyond borders, normality, the usual? Transcendence.

In fact, it's how we got here, crossing lines, sneaking past customs officers. Both of us countries on a map where the shorelines magically fit into each other, an isthmus into a bay.

Though I remain negative, I am becoming positive all the time, not in the cells of my blood or the hidden recesses of my brain, but in the way magnets change each other, the way electrical charges alter and become the same.

I celebrate masculinity. I saw a photo of your younger self and the face was round, like a boy's: the shapes of sun and moon and celestial bodies. Soft forms. Now the drugs have made your face gaunt, your cheekbones have risen like mornings and your cheeks have strong lines carved into them. I say this to you: You look like a man. Your profile is an exaggerated model, a cartoon superhero, sleek and virile. And strong like seaside cliffs that weather wind and salt night and day and all of the middle hours. A few of my body parts fit perfectly into those crevices.

For a time, the Crixivan causes your stomach to protrude, and I know this makes you shy in public. Ignore the wondering eyes. I see a yin to the yang. The roundness here softens the angle in your face. Your belly protrudes and gives birth to new forms, to all of your hopes and fears, to petty victories and multiplying neuroses. I run my hands over it and it is the shape a belly should be, a shallow overturned bowl of the finest cracked porcelain, a dark shade of ivory, coveted by the museum that guards it.

This month, I am fascinated by your veins, the way they stand out, the rivers and streams on your arms in shades of blue, the color of sensitivity and communication. I can see the way your blood reaches your fingers, which are warm when you touch me.

When you changed the combination of therapy, you lost weight. Now, you worry how thin you have become, about taking on skeletal form. The drugs waste your muscles. Fat flies off of you. It hurts to sit down for long periods because the bones in your buttocks are sharp. But look again in the mirror. Your body stretches up to the sky like a giraffe, you are lean like a gazelle, the sun on these African plains pleases you. Your flesh unencumbered is elegant, the body of dancers you have admired and here you are free of practise and training and a hundred painful jetés.

I hold you, you are light in my arms. Like cradling the skull of a newborn, a chick in the palm of your hand, a crystal glass between thumb and forefinger. You are so heady and soft that I drink you like champagne, or wine casked before the wars, so fine that it does not touch your throat on its way to your stomach.

How could I not want to make love to you? Like when the old down comforter split open under the rips of our passion and we had sex amidst feathers, a ghostly flock of ducks glad to bequeath us a backdrop. Our sweat and cum made the down stick together in soft clumps. Listen. If you were heavier, I would not have you. I have gotten used to this lack of gravity.

I love you for your vulnerability. Your body weak. From a cold made worse from a drug side effect, still the lingering cough? No, this time, it is the diarrhea, a river that doesn't stop, all of the insides pouring out and the drugs making you unable to hold in liquid or food. Out, it says. Expel.

I project a cradle around you to rock you into sleep, since I know you don't like to be touched when you feel like this. When I see you weak, I remember recovering from a flu, sitting on a high stool in grandmother's kitchen, sipping lemon and honey. I think of food that heals and I want to dissolve into herbs for you to taste and be surprised that I am aphrodisiac as well as medicine. Savor me from head to toe and I will enter you. Spice of life.

Sometimes, it is when you are weak that you are the hardest. Like the shell of an egg. We marvel at it, how thin yet tough, the sandpaper finish, how gently it carries its secret sun within. I would lift you into my jaw and carry you farther to a safer place. But you would not let me. Instead you are as hard and sharp as that shell.

When you are that brutal, my cock strains against the inside fabric of my underwear, the outline appears through pants or trousers or shorts. Your bravado titillates me. Your knife edge scares me. Shivers down my spine that reach down to the hairs between the cheeks of my buttocks.

Everyone fantasizes. Gay men are the best at it. As children, as a way to escape to someplace else; as adolescents, as a way to lose oneself en route to orgasm; as adults, habit. Gay men often fantasize about danger. The themes are leather, military, policemen, rough trade, construction workers, men who are powerful, who could overpower. Highway men who hold up fluorescent yellow signs that say hazardous, warning, harmful materials, slow down, stop. For years I envisioned binding, tying, overpowering those who taunted me, those I believed would taunt me. They would fall, simply, beneath my magic strength, and I would have my way with them. Before I knew what sex was, I would simply envision them straining and sweating, the muscles tensing in and out of sharp relief.

We flirt with danger. Does it flirt back? Why not flirt with what is really dangerous. The disease. That which has destroyed, taken lives, ravaged nations. So strong and powerful. Sexier because we cannot see it, and must picture it in our minds. Everyone is talking about it these days. The ads on Internet chat lines: barebacking, skin on skin, no protection.

It is amazing the lengths to which we go. Bungee jumping, hang gliding, parachuting, roller coasters. The ground beneath us is gone, replaced by a sense of velocity that would usually equal injury or death but somehow, here and now, we escape it.

Andy Quan

.....

So the ultimate turn-on is not skin and sweat or the symmetry of nipples. A physical touch that reminds you of the shock of how sweet and rich are the finest Belgian truffles and at the same time of that dizzy sharp edge of not eating for a full day. How hard kissing can be. A duet of tongues. Or how soft.

No, it's in the mind. An entire national library of the erotic. Here's the shelf on immortality, the invulnerability of the young or the want-to-be young. This is where you don't care. Where you do something that might kill you because the moment, or your imagination, or your just-fuck-it philosophy takes over. Indifference to consequence can be the sweetest part of the body.

Some more shelves: suicidal tendencies. Here's a book on how growing up in a disapproving society gives you low self-esteem, and how you might think you're not worthy enough to protect yourself. Play with fire but get burned. We can have the most passionate of fuck-sessions and then feel wrong. So much unreconciled. Repression breeds heat, which may just explode into passion. Are the religious books here too, the ones that say joy must be paid for by penalty? It's all the same category. How many of us negotiate disaster because we feel we deserve it? Put an end to our pale dreary lives. Gay men have always had a flair for drama.

The last stop on our tour, this section: sacrifice. The ultimate proof of love. I will do anything for you. There is nothing more powerful than to be inside you, for you to be inside me, to become each other. The model of twins rather than opposites attracting. I love you so much, I want you so much, I want to be you.

Of course, it manifests in a physical form. A shudder and

semen in its pearly white case of saltwater glue. You finger paint with it until it dries. Dirty pictures on flesh. But it all starts somewhere else. From the electrical charges and bytes and synapses of the brain that let you know it's in charge. The mind, not the body, creating sex, allowing it to happen, rigid, not flaccid.

I'm safe. Always. According to my rules, which are condoms and lube for fucking and being fucked. Oral OK. Rimming too, though only with the right asshole. But sometimes, I fantasize about being as dangerous as other men. Fantasy is part of the fun.

Listen, when it comes down to it, I desire you because you are dying. Men are taught to be protectors. No matter how much I have bucked the trends of what masculinity is supposed to be, I still picture myself on the white horse, I gallop past and sweep you into my arms, and you are no maiden, no lithe willow. You are a man. I picture fairy-tale sex, tragic romances, those trashy movies about people dying of terminal illnesses and I'm the star, I'm the one left behind, but before the big death scene the passion is incredible, it makes everyone in the movie house cry out from each sweat gland, they look like they're upset, but they're starting to writhe in sexual discomfort, or comfort, and when they reach out for the tissues, it's not just tears they're wiping away. We are having cinematic sex in Dolby sound and a clearer picture with more frames per second than ever before. The violins rise, fabrics billow, they've lit us so the room is dark but you can see each part of our excited bodies. Close-ups: my gasping open mouth; your hand on my nipple; the crack of your ass; my collarbone; your back, which looks like wings. The music gets louder and louder.

The woman who wrote it will win an Oscar. We're approaching climax and in this film, the cameras don't pan away.

No, I lie. It is because you cheat death. Because you are stronger than me. Because these days, the drugs are working, the T-cell count is fine, thank-you-very-much and the viral load is dropping, if you can count it at all. It's because you returned from that place and I catch you sometimes when you don't know I'm watching and you have this expression on your face that says you know a hell of a lot more than I do. You've glimpsed your own mortality and your eyes are lined, sometimes with dark patches beneath. Is this just some romance about those who have survived near-fatalities, not-so-terminal illnesses?

It is fact. You have taken stock of depths I can only guess at. You have prepared the true farewell speech, not some tragic teenage imagining *what would they do without me if...?* I am in awe of this. That you didn't turn to salt, or if you did, you became flesh again, pulled a few proteins and DNA out of the air, and the blood started to flow once more. I desire you because you are surviving, you are proud, you are living with it and me, it's a ménage à trois that works.

No, I lie again. I rub my brass genie-in-a-bottle cock and grant myself not three wishes, but three untruths that when discarded and retrieved and pieced together and seen in a different light may just tell more truth than I want to let be known. When it comes down to it, it is because of you, dangerous and beautiful, swelling to fill my mouth, pushing out against soft pink membranes and yellow-white enamel, the tiny slit at the end of your cock like an eye searching its way down my throat.

.....

Party Favors

Forget the setup: a scene crafted to tease you into the story; the establishing of character, place, emotional need, and time. Let's get to the point: men's sex parties—orgies—one to two hundred men at a time. Me as one of the participants. And up front, reasons for writing about them. *Because. Because* in a time when men have died from having sex with each other, we are finding ways to have sex. *Because* it is a hidden world that many, even gay men, do not know about. *Because* amidst the parts that are ugly, silly, mundane, or mean, there is caring and joy. *Because.* I was there.

When I first arrived in Sydney, I was lonely. It's not hard to meet people here but it's never easy to move to a new country. Belonging takes time. Luckily, Mardi Gras season offered many opportunities to socialize, and though I thought that the famous gay and lesbian event was only a big parade, it was actually a whole sequence of events—a number of small parties, a huge one, art exhibits, plays and concerts.

The pool party especially appealed to me: music and dancing around a public swimming pool. It promised a madcap water ballet with queer synchronized swimming, blow-up sharks and air mattresses, which the locals call *lie-lows*, men in women's swimming caps, women in men's lifeguard uniforms: all performed by volunteers.

I felt shy that night and there were few people I knew. A couple I did know had taken ecstasy pills and were soon in a different zone. Edgy and displaced, I found Don's frequent looks in my direction friendly, and his smile handsome and open.

A summary: we flirted, exchanged phone numbers, and made an arrangement to meet. It all turned out disastrously. I thought it hilarious and daring that we'd scheduled a precise time: four in the afternoon on a Thursday. He could only stay for an hour since he had to leave for another appointment. I told my flatmate at the time and, in fact, most of my friends. We all thought it was funny, and my only explanation was that he was a lawyer, and perhaps that's what they did. Scheduled in. But theory and practice did not mix. I felt rushed, the sex trivial. I was unable to become aroused at the ordained time and though I desired his body, particularly his strong chest, the sex was lackluster. However, instead of being forgotten in the annals of unmemorable trade, Don returns to me like a recurring dream. For it is to him that I trace my invitations to the parties of Sydney's Heavenly Orgy Team (HOT).

"There's an event I think you'll like," he told me. Though he got pretty much everything else wrong, on this assumption he was absolutely right.

The party was the day after Mardi Gras. Don had explained that he loved going to them but had to stop when he found a boyfriend who wanted to be exclusive, which didn't explain why he'd arranged to meet me. *Whatever.* He'd hinted at what was in store. Lots of men, and obviously, lots of sex. Oh, and nudity. You were required to take off all of your clothes. There would be a system.

The venue was a multistoried house with marble and glass surfaces emanating wealth. The front door opened to stairs leading up and down. Upstairs, I paid a small fee (to cover drinks, cleanup and supplies, they explained) and was given a white garbage bag with a number written on it.

"Go downstairs and grab yourself a drink," said a man with friendly eyes at the welcome desk. I walked down the stairs, through a large, open room, and then out of a wall of glass doors that led to a backyard with a small swimming pool and whirlpool, and a grassy area beyond that.

There were only about a dozen men there but it seemed to me a good scheme: to have a drink and a chat with people before things started, whatever those things might be. I asked men if they'd been to the party last night. They asked where I was from, whether I was visiting and if I'd come to live. This particular HOT party was renowned for bringing in out-of-towners; other parties would have a stronger local flavor. The parties traditionally followed Sydney's famous dance parties: Sleaze Ball, Mardi Gras, Inquisition, Hand in Hand, New Year's Pride. The day after these bacchanalian, communal gatherings of three- to twenty-thousand people of all shapes and sizes were smaller communal gatherings of more limited shapes and sizes and only of the male gender.

No one caught my eye in particular but I found the men friendly and fell into small summery chatter. The next time I looked up, the yard was full. The inside was filling up too. A loud voice called out instructions. I understood we were to crowd into the main room. We could barely fit in. Men spilled out onto the balcony.

"Welcome everyone, welcome to the annual Mardi Gras party of the Heavenly Orgy Team." A man was standing on a low stool so he was high enough to be heard. "We'd like to welcome all of our out-of-state and out-of-country visitors. We pride ourselves on being a group of men that are hot but warm, with no attitude, and welcoming to men from all cultures and countries. Remember, we have three rules here. One: total nudity. Two: safe sex always and three..." A weighty pause. "Say no politely, and yes enthusiastically." Some laughter. "Check-in is upstairs. Have a great party. Get your kit off!"

There was a smattering of applause and then confusion. Heads turned to watch others to try to figure out what next. I'd suddenly gotten nervous. Quite nervous. *Let's get this over with.* I made my way quickly through the crowd, slipped my clothes off and checked them in.

I'm neither comfortable nor uncomfortable with nudity but it's not my usual state. I felt a slight chill but was more aware of a barrage of internal voices as I descended the stairs, none of them intelligible. I couldn't guess what I was about to encounter. I was too jittery to be excited, too new at this for my heart not to be crashing around my ribcage.

My feet hit the cool marble of the floor, and in the middle of the room, the party had begun. Sunlight streaming in showered about forty men in light. I stepped into the crowd, which seemed to part, and without thought or anticipation, there was a man in front of me, short and well-built with the bluest eyes. We kissed only a moment before he broke off, leaned down and took my cock in his mouth. I hadn't noticed

I was hard but it was all happening at once. A tall man with a goatee leaned in to take over the kiss from the other man, and a dark Latin man, the same size as the first, was then at my left nipple: sweet, wet suction. The tall man bent down and took my other nipple in his mouth.

If anyone could have seen me, my eyes were as wide as planets. Amidst the physical sensation of three men pleasuring me at once, which I hadn't stopped to think had never happened before, clear words appeared in my head like a thought bubble in a superhero cartoon.

I'm not nervous at all.

And then: *I feel like a porn star.*

And then: *I am a porn star.*

The four of us were a tangle of appendages. Others moved in and the first man slipped away. In a breathing space where attention was on other men, I took a moment to look around. Crowded. Men everywhere. But there was space enough to move and the motion was fluid, gentle waves of flesh, men darting this way and that.

Unlike other times in my life when a restaurant menu confounds me, I became decisive. With this man, I shared a smile. I caressed this one's chest as he walked by, the shoulders of another. I was on my knees to interact with another. He beamed at me as he looked down, and stroked the top of my head gently. Another I embraced chest to chest. Someone else from behind.

We understood each other wordlessly. Before the party, I'd worried both about whether I would be rejected by some and whether I wouldn't be interested in others. But here, eyes met and we knew each other's thoughts. Eyes said yes, and we moved towards each other. Or accompanied by a slight nod, we acknowledged each other and passed by. How could anyone feel rejected by one man when there was another man waiting for him seconds away? I never quite believed the cliché, "there is someone for everyone." Yet here, it seemed, there was enough for all to share, and indeed, many someones for everyone.

I decided to explore. At the top of the stairs was a small alcove, two walls of concrete and one of glass. Here, two tall men had begun to kiss and embrace. One was blondish, stockier than the other. The other was who really caught my interest. From his profile in the act of kissing, I could see a powerful jawline, high cheekbones, large eyes with dark eyelashes. A swirl of wavy brown hair. He was tall with a long, lean muscularity. I could see it in the way the light caught lines in his back, shoulders, even his legs. Gay men have the habit these days of only working on their upper bodies, forgetting thighs and calves, but this body was symmetrical.

Had I ever been so bold? So confident to approach a man who looked like that? To think that my lust would be reciprocated, despite the fact he was already with someone else? But my brief transformation into a porn star downstairs had obviously upped my confidence. I approached them. They stopped what they were doing, and looked at me. The blond grabbed my cock, a bit roughly, and the dark-haired one put his hand around my shoulders and guided me close to them. He looked me directly in the eyes and though I've yet to experience it for real, I swear that I was parachuting out of a plane with something big and strong holding me aloft but all the blue sky and the lands below stretched out before me.

• • • • •

"You're beautiful," he said.

I'd describe the next minutes, the three of us in wild, panting heat, but the thing is, I've forgotten most of the detail. I'm sure it involved some stroking, kissing, embracing, and squeezing. At nearly all times, my body was touching two other bodies in one way or another. If I had been a computer, my hard drive would have been crashing.

After I did crash, my senses started to clear: the remnants of red wine being rinsed from a glass, the water and crystal becoming transparent again. I felt a chill, and noted our bodies covered in sweat. We looked at each other and at the floor covered in semen, and laughed. "I'll see if I can find something to wipe this up," one of them offered. Then I looked over my shoulder. The organizers' desk was set up immediately across from us. Two bemused men were staring in our direction. We had put on a show.

One grabbed a roll of paper towels to hand to the blond, and the other called me over. "Hey. Are you on the mailing list?" he asked. "Would you like to be on it?"

That was the way I got involved with the HOT parties, and it wasn't until much later, when I was helping with a mail-out, that I'd discovered my performance had gained me admirers. Most men received one invitation each. Invitations were hot items, exclusivity made them more so. But I'd received, and thought everyone on the mailing list received, five invitations. "You see," pointed out Charlie, who was in charge of the labels, "there's a little five in brackets here. That means we want you to invite your friends." He winked at me.

I was a regular at the parties over the next four years. The number of men increased each time, eventually pushing over the two hundred mark. The biggest problem the organizers had was finding a place to host the events. Even though they hired cleaners each time to leave the venues "cleaner than when we'd arrived," it was hard to find big spaces where furniture could be moved away, and that had showers and basins.

I used my invitations. I was too excited not to share the experience with friends. Many had heard rumors of HOT parties and some had gone over the previous five years or so. I ended up dividing men into three categories: Those who would never go. Those who were curious but undecided. Those who would go. These factors didn't seem to relate to any particular social factors or characteristics, to how much sex they had or how they found sex: saunas, parks, cruising areas, the Internet. The idea of a sex party appealed only to some.

If I did find a commonality among them, it was that, like the men who went to the parties, my friends who were interested were attractive but not stereotypically beautiful. I supposed those men might go to their own parties, though I thought it more likely that they were too worried about how they look and who they're attracting to really enjoy the benefits of an orgy. Besides, I think we were all proud that we weren't like the orgies we'd heard about in Los Angeles and other cities reserved only for the "beautiful." The men who went to HOT parties in Sydney were attractive in some way or another because they like sex. If you like sex too, you'd probably get along with them.

One year after my first party, the HOT event was taking place at the same huge house. I'd been to a few HOT parties in between, some better than others. I'd also discovered

• • • • •

Viagra. Well, not yet. My flatmate had sold me one, and I'd heard from friends who'd tried it that it was fun, and probably useful. "So, do you just get an erection and it lasts for twelve hours?" I'd asked, and Duane had explained that it just makes it easier to get erections. They last longer. They go away but come back quickly. "It's good," he told me. "Just don't do it with poppers. Your heart can stop."

I took the pill at a time calculated so I'd just be feeling it after clothes came off. But it worked quicker than I expected. When they called for "clothes off" I already had a raging hard-on in my pants. It didn't help that I'd noticed a short, muscular man that I'd seen at the party the night before. I hadn't felt particularly horny there—unusual considering I was surrounded by thousands of shirtless men. But out of the multitudes, he caught my eye in the corner of one of the dance halls. I'd tried for the longest time to get his attention but with no luck. And now, twelve hours later, he was here, with a chest so big it looked like it was going to fall over itself. He had smooth, creamy skin and a tiny mouth pinched into a shy smile. This time, he looked at me. I edged into the line a few men behind him, excited. Everyone had taken their clothes off already. I did the same. But there was no way to hide it. My erection was straight as a new ruler. Men walking by were staring. I was trying to decide whether I'd look stupid obscuring it slightly with my clothes, and then shook myself out of my mental chatter. *Show it proudly.*

By the time I'd checked my clothes in, my object of desire had disappeared. I didn't give it a second thought since I was in a state of disbelief that there were three men in the near vicinity that all fell into my definition of "muscle-god." I admit being muscle-fixated but I'm also attracted to different types. Over the course of a few parties, I seemed to develop themes. At one, I'd play with rough men with goatees. At another, blonds. Another party, I'd ended up in a foursome with two fit, slim Chinese boys and an Indian.

But this party, maybe the theme would be My Lucky Day. Could I play with these tall muscular men with defined physiques? I had worried at one time that my attractions were dictated by the imagery of gay books and magazines but I couldn't argue with my throat, dry with lust. I'd tried without luck to catch the eye of the redhead as we'd entered the party at the same time. Or was he a strawberry blond? It seemed somewhere in the middle, but I was more concerned with his skin, slightly freckled all over, and his rosy pink nipples, flat on a broad, full chest. Kent, I'd actually had sex with before. He was from Melbourne and had a strange, angular face: deep-set dark eyes below a shaved skull, high cheekbones, a long chin. His body was like those of bodybuilders in magazines, a boxy vascularity. Robin, I'd played with before too. Pale white skin, and dark, brown hair, with a short goatee. He looked like a statue of a Greek god both in face and physique.

When the redhead slid into place beside Robin, I strolled over. Robin grabbed my face and stuck his tongue in my mouth, a full, thick protrusion. Out of the corner of my eye, I saw that Kent had lined up next to the redhead. What surprised me, as I dropped to my knees, was that not only were the three men I was most attracted to at the party standing next to each other, but that no one else had joined in. I felt men watching me, and felt smug as I took Robin, then Kent, and then the redhead into my mouth, my hands dancing from cock to cock, squeezing balls with quick slides back up to their arseholes then up in front, the palms of my hands reaching up this wall of muscle, each of the three quite different from the other, and each a masturbatory fantasy. It also surprised me how passive they were: gently jerking each other off, hands feeling each other's torsos, and only a kiss here and there, not even a full lip-lock.

I wondered afterwards whether it had been too light, whether too many people were watching, or whether these three men were too inhibited by their own muscularity and beauty to let loose their full sexual energies. Maybe they weren't even that attracted to each other, they just thought they'd look good lined up like that. I certainly thought they did. Or maybe my teenage experiments with bending forks with the power of my mind had manifested in something much, much better.

I stopped to catch my breath and found my erection was still in full glory. *So, that's what Viagra does.* I felt someone standing at my side.

"You," he said.

"And you," I replied, surprised. "I haven't seen you since last year."

"Exactly one year ago. I remember you well." His gaze didn't falter. It was the striking dark-haired man from the three-way. "I don't live in Sydney, I just come in from Perth from time to time." Then he gestured with his eyes to my cock. "Nicc."

"I think I'm embarrassed."

"Don't be."

"I don't think we ever exchanged names."

"No. I don't think we ever did." He paused as if he wasn't going to tell me. "It's Justin."

Party Favors

.....

We walked outside together. I saw my friend Frank sitting down in the sun and went to say hello. Justin saw someone he knew. I noticed nearby a big, broad-shouldered man with a shaved head who was just standing up after being fucked. I looked at him in a stupor. Something about his thick torso and the size of him had ignited something inside of me. He looked at me lazily. Not in an unfriendly fashion.

I gestured to Frank, "hang on." I approached the stranger and felt the heat from his body standing next to mine. "Can I fuck you?" *Did I say that?*

"Sure. Yeah. OK." He started to lean over, put his hands on his knees. I hurriedly grabbed a bottle of lube and a condom from near the fence. *Kid in a candy store. Or bull in a china shop?* I wondered as I fumbled with the condom.

We heard a crashing sound from inside. A distraction. Someone laughed and I heard someone explain, "It's the lube on the marble floors, people keep on falling down the stairs." *Ouch!*

My sheathed cock slid in easily, and I hugged him from behind. He was warm as a sandy beach. Cuddly as the biggest teddy bear I'd ever owned. I stood on my tiptoes to try to get some leverage.

He looked up in front of him, and saw Frank. "Oh, hi Frank! How ya going? I haven't seen you since you lived in Wellington."

Frank looked surprised, than amused as he caught my eye, me humping and rocking back and forth in obvious excitement.

"Yeah. Things are good, Harvey." Frank was trying not to laugh. "Are you over for a few days, or longer?"

So, they chatted, as if over tea, while I was inside big Harvey, happy as Larry. (I don't really know who Larry is, but this Aussie phrase denotes contentment, and I was happy as a pig in slop.)

There was a sudden commotion. I stopped what I was doing. Frank and Harvey ceased talking. Someone was very excited, and getting louder, like the approach of a police car with sirens running. Higher in volume it went and everyone looked up and stopped what he was doing. It became silent except for a snigger here, a comment there. Then: *"OOOOOOOOOOOOHHHHH!"*

A veritable country yodel, a moose call, an "abandon ship."

Spontaneously, everyone clapped.

Sometime afterwards, in a scene that I'd tell my grandkids about, if my grandkids were gay sex-pigs, Justin and I entered the Jacuzzi at the same time as the short chesty guy who was my first obsession at this party. I'd managed to find out his name was Andrew and happily, he seemed interested in both of us. And proved it. We took turns kissing him, and then Justin and I linked arms under Andrew's shoulders. We held him up, the chlorine-blue water below bubbling like brew in a cauldron and his body floated straight out. He was short enough that he fit perfectly in the space. Floating above the surface was his massive chest; his tensed abdomen (water washing up and down the crevices like at an ocean's edge); and a small, put perfectly formed cock, straight, hard and delicious. We took turns tasting it, pre-cum mixed with pool water. We stroked and felt his weightless torso floating over the thrashing water. Finally, Justin grabbed his balls and I his penis and we kissed each other as we made Andrew come.

.....

As for us?

"What do you want to do?" Justin looked amused as he cast a glance over the crowd at the party.

"I want to take you home."

"That would be a pleasure."

"My Viagra is still working."

"Really?"

"Or maybe it's just you."

At my apartment, I was hungry not only for flesh. I wanted to know what made him tick. And lacking self-confidence, I wondered how such a beautiful man found me attractive.

"I used to live in London," he told me. A glint in his eye that I didn't understand. "I was with a lover there for fifteen years until he died." But he said this in an odd sort of way, as if there were something more. "You might know his name."

I did. It was someone famous who'd died of AIDS, so famous that to hint at it here would easily reveal his identity. "You were his lover?" Brushes of fame. Six degrees of separation. One degree closer to an infamous Englishman.

"Yeah. A lot of people asked me what I saw in him that was attractive. You know he wasn't an attractive man. But I thought so. It wasn't love at first sight, but when I got to know him, there was something very powerful. I loved him." Pensive for a second. "Still do."

Justin had worked as a model in London, part-time, a few big gigs here and there, but never too seriously. He knew famous people. He worked intermittently, though one of his main tasks in the last years was to take care of his dying partner.

I understood that Justin's concept of beauty was particular, and not ruled by what the wide world or the gay world thought. It was, for me, a marvel that this man, perhaps as handsome as I'd ever seen, had found me amongst two hundred men and thought me as beautiful as I did him. Over the next two years, Justin called me when he visited Sydney and we got together for mind-blowing, gasping, electrifying sex. Then he got a job requiring him to travel mostly in Asia and stopped coming to Sydney. We keep in touch by e-mail.

A year later in a small, dark terrace house, I was in a reflective mood. The parties weren't always so good. The energy at smaller ones sometimes didn't take off. The venues could be cramped, or dark, or lacking in some way. After the first HOT party, where I'd found the atmosphere respectful, I found if it was too crowded or dark, men took more liberties. Grabbed before they asked. Felt before making eye contact.

At this party, I had noticed an older man watching me. He had thick curly dark hair and a walrus moustache. He was hairy and overweight in a way that I did not find attractive. I didn't pay him much attention though I had returned his smile to be friendly. I hadn't spotted many prospects though. The edgy thrill of these events, I had to admit, had worn considerably since the first parties where not only had I felt the spark of the new, but had learned that *being* new had had its advantages. There was a core group of men that go to HOT parties, and upon arriving at each additional party, my sexual radar (the one that told me where the men I was most attracted to were in the room) pointed me to men I'd already had sex with, or who I knew from past experience weren't interested in me. It was the same for others—I'd notice them look my way immediately and think, *Oh, I've done him.*

It was the same at this party, as I scanned the room for someone fresh, and felt cynical doing so. I've learned that I find sex the most exciting when it is with a complete stranger, or with someone I know well, a lover or boyfriend. So, looking around at all these not-quite-strangers, I thought, *maybe it's time for a bit of a break.* Richard, though, was an Asian man with a long torso and stomach muscles like dominoes stacked from his chest to groin. Brent was his white equivalent: a body, I found out later, built through years of cycling. When they gestured for me to join them, some chamber of my mind echoed *thank you thank you thank you.*

I sucked on Brent's nipples, which stuck out appealingly, and then stood up to kiss Richard. Brent kneeled to suck my cock (so warm and wet, was the shape of his mouth and throat a perfect fit, or was it just good technique?). A thin, young guy then joined us too, switching from another group of men to us. One of my arms was around him and the other around Richard.

And then I felt it. Unmistakable. A walrus moustache in the crack of my arse, a scratchy cat's tongue rolling around my anus. I was being rimmed by the older man. I tried to let other sensations take over. Lips on my nipple. A lolling tongue-kiss. Brent's excellent blow job. My hands on torsos that I found beautiful. But I still felt the brush of facial hair in my arse and an unwanted visitor. I was helpless. My hands were full and my lips engaged. I couldn't even turn my head. Eventually, the rimming stopped and soon after, the group of us all came, a staggered symphony of groans and grunts. Before I left the party, Walrus Man caught my eye from across the room and winked.

At the following party, I pointed out Walrus Man discreetly to friends. "Look, if you see that man coming for my arse with his tongue, can you run up as if I'm the most attractive man you've ever seen and pretend to fuck me?" They laughed and agreed, but not more than halfway through the party, he'd caught me again. It was obviously a calculated technique. He waited until I was lost in a scene with my hands full but my arse uncovered and shot in like a swallow into a barn.

I remembered this particular party for two other reasons. The first, I never found out his name. Everyone had noticed him though: his dark looks, clipped body hair (unusual since most men were still shaving themselves smooth) and an exquisite athletic form with a back the shape of a flock of birds heading south. He could have been Spanish, or Greek, or Latin American, it was hard to say, though the accent I overheard was pure Aussie. But if you ever had a Ricky Martin fantasy—this guy had him beat.

He was with another young man, slim and blond, who was more boisterous. "C'mon," I heard him say to the dark-looking gymnast as he moved through the crowd in the direction of a balcony. I think the blond was on some party drug; he had that frenetic energy, and as he passed by me, he reached back his hand and grabbed on to mine instead of the gymnast's. I allowed myself to be led and when he stopped and turned around, he only looked faintly surprised. Gymnast appeared from behind me and the three of us started having sex. I remember him not only for his dark beauty but because when he turned the other man around and put his cock into him, I stroked his back from his nape down to his arsehole and found it sticky with lube. I took it as an invitation, especially since it allowed me to feel the strength of his torso from behind as he was fucking the blond against the balcony. I put on a condom, lubed up and entered him, and we found a surprisingly graceful motion, the three of us. I'd never before fucked anyone while that person was fucking someone else. Something new every party.

A few months later, I saw him at a nightclub event with friends. I regularly see men around town that I recognize from the HOT parties. I tend to greet them in a friendly way and if anyone asks, say that I "met them at a party." Everyone in Sydney meets people at parties.

I didn't recognize at first though that this is where I'd met him. He had clothes on and was moving differently in this environment. But I couldn't keep my eyes off of his handsome face. Finally, I caught a freeze-frame of him in a pose that was familiar. Now, I remembered. When he passed by later, I said hello. He gave me such a questioning look, I felt obliged to explain: "I thought I'd met you somewhere."

"No." His disdain dripped off his tongue. He tossed his head back slightly and laughed as he walked off.

It was so vehement, I questioned for a second whether I was right or not. But as he strode away I recognized his form even through his clothes because I'd known his body. My eyes bored into his back.

I was inside you.

The other acquaintance from that party was much more cordial. Brad was over six feet tall. Bald with a goatee. A wide bear of a man with a thick chest, big nipples, and strong thighs. I recognized him from one of the gay Internet sites.

Andy Quan

.....

He looked exactly like his photos and was as big as I'd expected. But his smile in person was even broader.

He strode into the center of the room, went up to another man, and started kissing him with such intensity that everyone looked up. You could feel sexual energy emanating from him and out to the corners of the room. The level of intensity rose in all encounters. A few other men started to gather around him to feel his heat. He seemed oblivious, focused on the other, smaller man. You know when someone grabs your face with both hands to kiss you? Brad was so big that it seemed he was doing the same to the other man, except instead of just his face, he was grabbing his whole body as if lifting him up to draw him further into his mouth. Just by watching, I was becoming more and more horny. I moved into the group. I reached up and touched Brad's chest. He swung around, grabbed me around the waist, and locked mouths with me with the same intensity as he had the other man.

I like men of all sizes. Shorter than me, the same size, taller. Tall and lanky. Short and broad. But I loved being held by someone so big, my fingers tweaking his fleshy nipples, fondling his hefty cock and balls. It was a little unexpected too. I somehow hadn't imagine that his type, whatever he was—bear, muscleman—would be attracted to me—small (in comparison to him), fit but not too muscular, Asian. The categories all seemed to disappear with his thick tongue in my mouth. We couldn't stop kissing and didn't let go for an instant while we embraced and rocked back and forth and squeezed thighs, torso, waist, chest. Stroking each other's cock then another part of the body then back to cock, each time a little harder, tenser, ready to spring. Pre-cum leaked from both of our dicks.

A layer of sweat was forming all over his body, and starting to cover me as well. I noticed that I was becoming as loud as him, with uninhibited moans and gasps of pleasure and then his great bulk shuddered, and I did too, and we ejaculated upwards onto each other's hands, stomach, chest.

We drew apart and his smile was as wide as a boat. With my fingers, I worked his cum into his sweat and the hairs on his chest until it seemed to disappear. Instead of leaving each other, we sat down on the couch at the side of the room. "My partner would love you," he told me. He was still breathing heavily, his body winding down.

"Really?" I feigned ignorance but I'd seen his profile up on the Web too. They were a prominent couple. Brendan was a short bodybuilder with a rough, handsome face. I'd lusted after his photos but never dreamed he'd be interested in me, especially considering the looks of his partner.

"Oh, you are just his type."

"How about both of you together?"

"Brendan and I usually don't do threesomes," he shrugged. "Maybe we'll make an exception for you. But first, I think he'd probably want to just see you."

We arranged to e-mail each other details, and a few weeks later, another fantasy came true, and another lesson was learned: my preconception about who is attracted to me is not always true. How is it that we learn to limit ourselves so easily?

Brad went for a shower. I decided to get water from the kitchen. It was enough for me, this surprise gift. I thought it was time to go home. Leaning against the counter in the kitchen was a man with a slim build and sharp facial features:

nose and chin and cheekbones. Somehow I sensed that he'd not had much success at the party tonight. As I turned away from the sink, he slid in front of me, put his arms around me lightly and leaned in to kiss me. I reached my arm out to find somewhere to put down my water glass, and let him continue.

He was not a bad kisser nor was he unattractive. I was sated at that time but I thought at that moment, as he was getting more and more aroused, kneading the head of his penis: *He needs this. Shouldn't I oblige, as other men have done for me?* I relaxed my body, breathed deeply and imagined myself having sex with Brad only moments before, drawing on that uninhibited lust and horniness. I took quicker breaths and made sounds as if I was into this man as much as he was into me. He was grabbing more of his penis now, stroking the whole length then rubbing the head with his thumb. I spit into my palm and lent a hand, wetting his nipple on the way down. It didn't take long for him to come as he let go a sigh of relief.

"I needed that." He leaned his forehead into mine and gave my shoulders a squeeze. "Thank you."

"You're welcome. See you." I walked away to retrieve my clothes, happy to have done him this favor. A party favor.

The last of these events I went to was my fourth Mardi Gras HOT party. Two weeks before, I'd met Bruno, the man who would become my boyfriend, and I'd asked him along. With a sexual history like mine, I figured that our relationship could be many things but sexually exclusive would not be one of them. Considering that I'd met him in the middle of a sex space at the pre-Mardi Gras Speedos party, I figured he understood.

Party Favors

.....

As it happened, he'd already been invited to the party.

The organizers had lost their usual setting, the magnificent house. This party was held in a much smaller place with a good-sized outdoors area surrounded by fences, the furniture cleared out of the rooms inside. By now, I'd been to so many HOT parties that they were just as much a chance to catch up with friends as a chance for hot, group sex. I'd become friends with men I'd had sex with and friends with those I hadn't, as well as having introduced various friends to the parties. It was, at the beginning, necessary to get over any embarrassment or shame of seeing each other naked or indeed, sucking or fucking in front of each other. Once, I was being given a blow job while leaning up against some sort of gymnastic apparatus. I looked down and saw that a friend had his head sideways on a cushion below me. He was being fucked vigorously. He grinned and gave me a thumbs-up. At orgies, you see friends in a different light.

I saw a number of people I knew and introduced them to Bruno. I wasn't much in a sexual mood; maybe I was too tired from dancing the whole night before. An old acquaintance passed by and grabbed me into a tongue-kiss. I kneaded the muscles of his arse with my hands. Bruno didn't join in, and we ended up playing separately at that party rather than together. Still, I enjoyed seeing what type of men he moved between—more hairy, more manly men than I usually went for.

Bruno decided after a short time that he was tired, and that since we'd only been together for a short time, he only had eyes for me. Surrounded by two hundred men and I was the only one who made him hard: did I feel flattered or pressured? "Have fun!" he encouraged before he left.

.....

Bruno gone, I looked around. I saw many familiar faces though the bodies didn't necessarily match up. It amazes me how men in Sydney change their physiques like fashion, different clothes for different seasons. Someone will show up newly muscular or thin, or less defined with more weight. Rajan, the handsome Indian, had lost weight; Mikhael, the leatherman, had put some on; and Adrian, the silver fox, must be going to the gym a lot. As for the ones who'd been out dancing straight through for nearly a day: they had tired faces but looking at their bodies, it was as if a thin layer of fat had been stripped off like gift wrapping revealing grids of definition. Even my body was altered. I'd been cycling a lot at the time, and the night of partying had left me with abdominal muscles that I'd rarely seen.

My friend Archie has the habit of telling me each time I see him that he's met "the most beautiful boy he's ever seen." I find it irritating since his perspective seems affected by the moment rather than a broad history, and I don't trust those who forget the past so easily. But the HOT parties have made me more understanding of his vision. Every party, I did see extraordinarily handsome men, and more so, something special in each person.

These parties have taught me a lot. I've found that my sexual tastes are more varied than I think, and that tastes can change. Or moods: someone might chase me around the room at one party and be uninterested at the next one. I've learned to relax into the moment: let go of past expectations, but not fall too quickly into the future. I've learned to make my own judgments. I've heard detractors talk about group sex as being impersonal, but I found it very personal. By seeing many men instead of one, you can compare them and find different things sexy about each one. The strength of someone's back. The soft color of another's eyes. Most of all, I've become so much more confident. Through the power of men's desire for me. And mine for them.

In the end, this last night was more thoughtful than sexual. I played only with a few men, there were no big scenes for me. I was happy that I'd come to the party and was hesitating before leaving. I still wanted something. That person turned out to be a tall, slim, muscular man with his wavy hair tinted white-blond. He had high cheekbones and beautiful eyes and we laughed to find out that we were both from Toronto and we'd both come so far to be fucking each other in Sydney. He reminded me of someone. I fucked him from behind, first, and felt the long sinewy muscles of his back, and admired his straining thigh and calf muscles. Then we faced each other, my back propped up against a wall, him leaning into me as we kissed and jerked off and I traced the lines of his defined torso with my fingers.

Justin. He looks like Justin.

If Justin could not be here—he was probably having a quiet early evening in Perth with his partner—then I would make love to his look-alike, my friendly fellow countryman, whose face was flushing in the most attractive way as he was coming closer to ejaculation. We looked each other intently in the eyes before I leaned in to kiss him and wondered if he too felt like we were falling through the sky.

.....

Something about Muscle

Gay men can be as competitive and nasty as any other sexuality and gender but it takes its own form. A philosophy. Men I hate: those who attract with barely an effort men to whom they are attracted themselves. Men I feel sorry for: those who cannot attract the ones to whom they are attracted. As for those who attract guys to whom they are not attracted: *Whatever. Run faster.*

Me, I generally feel sorry for, but pretend I don't, or at least, I don't make it public. So, when I was changing out of my sweaty gym gear in the locker room of Urban Fitness and noticed in the corner of my vision what I thought was a man looking at me, a man who seemed to have very big muscles albeit on a short frame, I thought, *Nah. This doesn't happen to me*. And when he looked again, and I was suddenly sure that he was looking at me even though I was too surprised and nervous to meet his eyes, I remembered my philosophy and said to myself with a wry grin, "I hate you." I think he saw me smiling to myself, which I considered not a bad thing—without even trying, I had let him know that 1) I'd noticed his stare, and 2) I was very pleased with myself. Who cares that I was changing to go, and he was getting into his gear. I'm sure

I could figure it out!

He exited before me, and left me wondering if I was going to have to find him among the maze of equipment and then actually go up and make it look natural that I had something to say to him. But I didn't have to worry. He was waiting for me in the stairwell.

I won't bother recounting the introduction, because they're all the same. You can imagine it: greeting, returned greeting, innocuous question, maybe a comment, reply to said question-comment, volley, return-volley and so forth. Match point. Game! This one ended quickly, easily, and successfully: useful information, good news, and a phone number.

The useful information was his name, Morgan, and his occupation, house-painter (I like to know what people do). The good news was that he lived a block away from me and it sounded like arranging a meeting would be simple. And the phone number: eight digits in Sydney, starting with a nine, maybe an eight.

I walked home, still taking in his physical appearance. He was older than most men I looked at. A settled ruggedness. A spiderweb of lines at the corners of his eyes. His lips had an odd wrinkled fullness about them. His muscularity was sinewy, defined and large. My glimpse of him in the changing room was of something I'd fantasized about. He'd spent time in the sun, maybe too much time—Aussies are prone to skin cancer—and his skin was a ruddy tan color. He was either the same height, or shorter than me: five-eight, I'd guess.

That night, I let his image fill my head and jacked off, coming almost immediately.

Andy Quan

.....

I date my fascination with muscle to my childhood. I remember that documentary on Arnold Schwarzenegger called *Pumping Iron*. Various bodybuilding competitions on television. The best were the homegrown varieties. British Columbia's Provincial Championships, which I think I only caught twice, had camera work much closer-up, and the men in their variations from short to awfully big seemed more real, their coloring more natural than the oily tans illuminated by the bright spotlights I remember from Mr. Olympia and Mr. America.

No one required me to say why these men attracted me, so I never questioned it. Just watched with amazement the patterns made when different poses were flexed, the differences between the men themselves, this gift of near-naked men on display in my own living room, a room of my childhood.

I almost got started myself in high school. Two classmates had joined a brand-new slick fitness center that had opened up in our neighborhood. Athletic teenagers, they made quick gains.

"It's great," said Mini, short for Minotti, a muscly runt of an Italian. "Give it a try."

I went for a visit, during which an enthusiastic fitness instructor expostulated on the benefits of free weights over machines and a slightly disinterested promotions manager (but also fit, tall and strong) tried to convince me of the benefits.

"We'd fill in these parts here." He pointed to and touched lightly the indentations above my collarbone. My heart pounded wildly. *When could I join?*

Having no income at fifteen except a weekly allowance, I had to ask my parents. Would they help me? I had no idea since I generally asked little from them.

"Would you really use it?" asked my father who was not an athletic man. "I can't see you going."

"And what about school?" added my mother. "You've got a few months, and then summer, and then a new year. The membership is for a year. Do you know you're going to use it that long?"

At the time, the answer was no. I didn't know so I didn't argue. But now: of course I would have gone. And I probably would have even used the weights.

My attraction to muscle continued, but became more realistic. When I finally did start to go to the gym while in university, I learned how long it took to build up those comic-book muscles of competitions. I suddenly could tell which men worked out and which didn't and that the vast majority of regular fitness buffs didn't look anything like the men of my fantasies.

Through my twenties, I cultivated a lust for more regularly athletic bodies and tried to tuck away my hot panting tongue for the overblown and defined.

This situation was suddenly confused upon arriving in Sydney in 1999. My neck, used to gently turning from occasional glances at cute muscle boys, became strained from overuse and sudden craning. The flirtatious gay physiotherapist said it was a repetitive injury exacerbated possibly by a sharp, quick movement. "What sports are you doing?"

"Maybe something during my weight training," I lied.

But Sweet Mother of God. How could I not look at the sudden blooming of my fantasies before my very eyes? Hot weather and the muscles just grew and grew. Sydney was a town of gym queens and *Muscle Marys*, a phrase I first heard in London. Did the strongest people from all the country migrate to this one spot and breed? Was it because of the beach culture? A local shortage of fabrics? Plain, dumb (but pretty) luck? Or some regulation about being gay? *You must work out.*

Gay men were bodacious, bionic and Barbie-onic.

Not only that but during the famous dance parties—Sleaze, Mardi Gras and more—musclemen from around the world would descend on this one place—from London, Singapore, New York and Boston, Montreal and L.A.

Could I have sex with one of them? Could I fulfill my fantasy?

The problem was that while I went to the gym and played sport, I could never muster up quite enough hours—all the hours one needs to become a Muscle Mary. And most Muscle Marys seemed to only be attracted to each other. It was the *homo* part of the word *homosexual* taken to a new level.

The other question I couldn't shake off was whether it wouldn't matter if I worked out every minute of the day. That ever-growing perfect body would be passed over because it was Asian and not a white one. I'd seen it happen before and knew it wasn't my imagination. Those of us on the bottom rungs of the ladder know who is on top while those higher up are probably just staring at the view.

Still, I don't think about these things at all when I'm off my face, and once, on some miscellaneous dance party substance at some miscellaneous dance party, I wandered right into a towering six-foot-five mass of muscle, handsome too, but it was hard to notice his face with so many contours before me: biceps, chest, abdominals.

"Sorry," and then I saw what I'd bumped into. "Can I have a hug?" My request clear above the music.

.....

"Sure..." he replied in an accent I thought was American South. He enveloped me in that flesh and I was momentarily in the most amazing gay womb I could imagine.

Morgan rang me into his apartment, his voice scratchy through the security system. "Second floor, on the left, number sixteen."

He opened the door. I was nervous. Wondering what would do me more good in this situation: more muscle or more confidence? The entranceway opened directly into the whole split-level apartment; a flight of stairs led from an open kitchen to the bedroom below. I stood uncomfortably in the kitchen. We edged around each other, boxer's steps, until he finally leaned against the counter.

Business was good, he said and I could see that. It was his apartment, and property is expensive in Sydney. I wondered how many houses he had to paint to buy it. And if it was this constant, physical work that kept him so strong.

"What do you do?" he asked but wasn't really interested. "So, are we going to do anything?"

I took this as an invitation but still approached him as if he would either bite me, or run away. I placed my left hand on a shoulder as hard as—even harder than—I expected and leaned over to kiss him. He turned his head and I ended up nuzzling his neck and ear.

"C'mon, mate." He led me down the stairs.

I pushed him onto the bed, and lay on top of him still aiming for a kiss. He writhed below me, and his body was like nothing I'd felt before, as if it wasn't one piece but many pieces moving and shifting in different relation to each other.

.....

"This is different," he said.

Different from what?

He let me into his mouth but I wasn't paying attention by then, frankly. My hands were roaming his body, exploring. He had those big winged muscles under the arms that curve from the back to the top of the stomach. His pectorals, showing through his shirt, were perfectly parted with a ridged indentation in between them like the spine of a small animal. I slipped my hand beneath his T-shirt and up onto his back. It was volcanic, like molten ash hardened into ridges and contours, still warm.

I threw off my shirt, hurriedly, awkwardly.

"You're bigger than I thought you were," he commented.

Wait until you see my cock, I thought but furrowed my brow. He sounded surprised instead of excited. I grabbed his T-shirt and pulled upwards. He collaborated and lifted his arms up and the shirt came off in one motion. I gasped. His body was as I remembered it, round muscles defined with sharp lines. But maybe even more beautiful. I buried my head in them like a pig in slop, like some human food contest, my hands tied behind my back, gluttonizing on Jell-O, spaghetti, a giant chocolate sundae. The soft edible bits all consumed and my tongue now scraping the bottom of the bowl: hard rounded glass.

His nipples were especially delicious, neither tiny nor large. Still, they stuck out, rubbery offerings with just enough give in them to suck and nibble while he continued squirming below me like a snake shedding a skin. His blue jeans came off, then my army shorts. His hand went to my underwear, the outline of my cock. He pulled at the waistband with his index finger and looked inside.

Something about Muscle

• • • • •

"You're big. I haven't seen an Asian with a cock like this."

I would have taken it as misguided flattery but it wasn't. His comment had authority but wanted no favor. He grabbed the long shaft of my penis and started pumping rhythmically. I reached over to reciprocate, and felt the texture of his balls, relaxed and giving. They spilled out of my palm perfectly. His cock was a small, fat sausage—warm, but not erect. I stepped off the bed, grabbed his jock by the waistband and hauled it off, lifting his legs into a pair of scissors.

"This is different."

I dived down onto his groin and enveloped his cock with my mouth. I rolled it around with my tongue and felt blood filling the chambers. I reached up my arms to run down his torso. This to me was the most amazing part of Morgan's body. His stomach was like the underside of a tortoise shell. Each section was a plate of armor welded into place, side by side, perfectly arranged. It actually stood out from the rest of his body. His chest muscles were big and round enough to jut out past his abdomen. But unlike other men I'd seen whose midsections dipped, slightly concave like a cracked bowl, or most other men whose stomachs flattened, if they were lucky, but mostly softened, Morgan's was hard and convex. Just putting my hand on it sent electric pulses racing between my shoulders and groin and ricocheting in between.

My hand reached around to his arse. I didn't even think about it. It just slid around his hard buttocks and through his legs. I paused from sucking to spit on my finger, and returned to match the rhythm of my blow job with my finger sliding into his anus simultaneously. It slipped into an easy tight spot like a London driver squeezing into parking in the center of the city. He groaned, the loudest sound that I'd heard him make so far. I continued for a few seconds then worked my way up with my mouth through crevices and pathways like a maze, though I knew I wouldn't get lost.

Again: face to face. His features were old in this light and there again, his chapped lips. Did he lick them all day long? He was still only semierect.

"Sorry. I'm a little nervous tonight."

I'm too filled with lust to worry why he's nervous, or wonder if he's not attracted to me. I'm horny, selfish, and can't even breathe calmly. I shift behind him. I want to feel what it's like to hold him from behind and I bite his neck and squeeze his chest hard.

"This is different."

Then I can't help myself, it's my tongue being dragged through the labyrinth again to end up at the exit or entrance, a round hole, a radius, arrows pointing in or out and my tongue fits in perfectly where my finger was earlier.

It's hard to decide whether to place my hands on his back, sides, or legs—they're all rippling in different but intriguing ways—or do I just part his buttocks like the Red Sea and walk and walk and walk? Continuing with the theme of gluttony, I decide to do a bit of each.

"There's rubbers over there," he points.

Did I hear right? It's like an invitation to a restaurant I didn't think I could afford. True, he's not going to fuck me with a half-limp dick and I'm glad for that since I'm an awkward bottom. But this is unexpected. Unexpectedly good.

I reach over. There are condoms and sachets of lube in a drawer. I grab one, rip it open, and take a few lube packets in the other hand. I wish there was a dispenser instead of these fiddly free things. He's still on his stomach, just lying there, kind of looking back to watch me.

"I might be a little tight."

But I've got the rubber on, and have slathered two sachets of jelly up and down my shaft and the remainder on his asshole. My cock slides into his asshole in two stages, just a short pause after the first, and then it's all the way in, and he's writhing and twisting beneath me.

My hands are on his stomach from behind him and it feels like I'm gripping the bar of a roller coaster and my stomach is lurching with excitement and exhilaration. I'm sitting (kneeling actually) bolt upright but the world is whooshing past me sending things in and out of focus.

It suddenly strikes me, the image I'm looking for. He's some sort of arthropod, the 90 percent of the animal kingdom that wears its skeleton on the outside of its body. Like the plates of a prawn or lobster. I know: not very erotic until you tear it open and suck the sweet flesh right out. But the hard moving parts are like no human I've touched, and somehow I like it. How am I going to recreate this?

I'm mostly just riding him, my cock as far inside of him as it will go when I feel a spasm, that little signal that my excitement is boiling over:

No, I don't want it to happen. I've been fucking him for no longer than two minutes. Shit! I'm too excited, this is too exciting, I—Ai—Ay. Ohh.

My body shudders, I can't pretend anything else is happening than an orgasm. The last bit of jizz shoots out of me and into the condom and there's a sudden drop of temperature as if the sun has ducked behind a cloud.

"That was quick."

"Sorry. Uh, do you want to come?"

"No, mate." His body is covered in a thin coat of sweat. He looks down at his dick. "I don't know what's wrong with it tonight."

I consider kissing him again but think better of it. He's not much for kissing.

"When I saw you in the gym, I didn't think you were so big."

"Really?"

"I usually go for guys thinner than you. Not so muscular."

I picture myself as a woolly mammoth. "Is that your boyfriend?" I've spotted a photo of two people on his dresser.

"Yeah, I have a boyfriend."

Things are becoming clearer.

"He lives with his parents out in Parramatta. He comes in one night a week—on Thursdays and then on Saturday."

"Can I have a shower?"

I shower with Morgan. I soap his body down front and back, my hands up and down his legs. It's quick, he submits but does not let himself go.

So, that was what was different. A muscular Asian boy, aggressive with a long cock. Who fucked him. Not a young, slight, passive Asian boy who lives with his parents. *That was different.*

I know I shouldn't push it. I want more, and I know that to get more, the key is to play it cool. Yet he invited me to call him again, and I will.

Something about Muscle

.....

I'm away on a work trip for two weeks. This gives me ample time to pretend I'm more casual about it than I am. Casual is *not* jacking off every night fantasizing about fucking him again. I dream of no early ejaculation for me, and a hard dick for him. A proper fuck-session, if I can control myself. If I can't, maybe he'll let me practise.

I can tell he's not a phone person when I call him. The conversation is curt and to the point and I can't ascertain from the tone of his voice whether he's happy to hear from me.

"Monday," he says, disappointing me, since it's Wednesday. "I'll be free on Monday night. Call after work."

I figure it's not a good idea to look a gift horse in the mouth. Maybe someone horse-hung, but in that situation it would be your mouth you'd be concentrating on, not his.

I spend five days and five nights in a pent-up state. I'm horny and I want sex, but I've decided who I want sex with. I try to decide whether to call another man with whom I'd had sex the month before, but it's only Morgan who's going to scratch this itch. As well, I'm finding it hard settling into the new city. No boyfriends in sight. Not enough friends. Work is stressing me out. I want a fuck. I want Morgan. I want to lose myself in his muscles.

On Monday I wait all day and then some more. I radiate anticipation, so much that my flatmate walks by and asks me if I'm arranging some trade.

"Hope so," I reply and dial the number.

It rings. And rings. After the seventh tone, the answering machine clicks in. It's his same gruff voice and a nondescript message.

"Hey, Morgan. Give me a call when you get in." I leave

my phone number. Then, I pace around, decide to make dinner, make dinner and wolf it down as quickly as possible in case he calls, and to try to give myself time to digest it.

I call again. This is the message I leave. "Hey, Morgan. I thought we were supposed to get together tonight. Give me a call." I'm edgy now. I'm bad enough when something I've planned to do in the evening falls apart. It's not that I don't like spending time alone, but when I plan to see or do something, I psyche myself up to do it and find it hard to redirect my energy. And I hate that I don't have friends yet who I can call any time, and say, *Hey, I'm bored, let's go out for a drink.*

It's worse that I've been stood up a few times lately by acquaintances. It's this new-guy-in-town thing: it's up to me to find their rhythms, fit into their schedules, make the proposal and double-check the date. That's what I don't always do—double-check—which leaves me with evenings yawning and stretching their way out before me, taunting me to fill them with something different than going to sleep early and jacking off.

Where is he? Fuck.

I go out for a walk. I have nothing to do. I consider dropping by his place, but can't remember the apartment number, and even if I did, I know it would be the wrong thing to do. When I return to my apartment, it's late, but not too late to fuck, and still too early to sleep. I leave one last message:

Sorry we couldn't catch up tonight. I'll call again sometime to find out when you're free.

Two days later I'm still burning with lust and frustration. I call. "Hi Morgan, it's..." He hangs up. Wait. Did that just happen? I call again and the line is busy.

Something about Muscle

.....

It's two weeks later when I run into him on the street. He pauses, and I can feel his anger. He doesn't know whether to walk right by or not.

"Look Morgan. Whatever it is, I'm sorry, can you tell me..." I've picked up this righteous tone in my voice.

"He was there."

I shut up. I swallow.

"He heard the messages."

It sinks in what happened.

"I had to tell him."

It sinks in what I've done. "I..." I fix him with a stare, and no longer see the bodybuilder of my dreams. I see an upset older man with a terrific body who is not much of a talker and wants to get away from me as soon as possible.

"I'm sorry, Morgan. It was stupid of me to do that. I won't call again."

He grumbles something that I take as consent and I watch him walk away, his footsteps resigned and sad. I feel my long rubber-sheathed cock up his muscular arse, my hands at the top of his armor of stomach muscles, and the calamity of movement below me as his musculature shifts back and forth between the four directions. I make a note to myself to try to hang on to this physical memory for as long as I can because I know it's the last I'll ever feel of it.

.....

Getting It If You're Asian

You're born. You slide out of your mother's sex, oblivious to her pain, and covered with the memory of your father's sex inside that cavern nine months before, give or take a little depending on whether you're premature—pounding your clenched knuckles out into the world saying *let me out let me out*—or late, wanting a bit more of that embryonic pillow, a touch more shut-eye.

The years afterwards fly by without too much importance until the body's chemistry signals it to change into a new form. You get acne and oily skin and wonder years later why people insist that as an Asian you have a perfect complexion. Then the harder part, and softer ones too. You become man. You become woman.

The question (for now at least, not the only question, just one of the questions but not a bad one to focus on) is: How do you get it? How do you go about getting it?

First, check out your lineage. Were your parents the kind that never talked about it? Did they ever show physical affection in front of you? Did they do ballroom dancing in the living room and cha-cha-cha in the bedroom? Make the bedsprings creak? Were they actually having a lot more of it than you ever knew about? Sorry for bringing that up.

But it is an important consideration. A happy marriage can be a good model for a happy partnership which might include a good deal of it. Feuding parents, on the other hand, might mean that when you have it, it's brutal, distant and filled with fears of betrayal and abandonment. Horny parents might mean you're comfortable with your body and you might be an early bloomer yourself. Shy parents might mean it might take you forever to get it. You might not even know that you want it.

A close family might mean your need for it gets replaced by this big kind of *Brady Bunch* feeling and you don't really have time to think much about it, because you're permanently locked into the role of Marcia, Jan, Cindy, Greg, Peter or Bobby. Only Asian. A close family might mean a lack of space and opportunity since when are you going to get it when you'll live at home until you're thirty and maybe you share a room.

If your family is too close, it might drive you away. It might make you become that bad girl or boy they fear, delving into it like a teenager into a mosh pit. You differentiate yourself from your parents by giving in to something alien to their chaste worlds. You try perfume but give it up, hoping you'll smell of what you're doing, the scent a little different with each partner.

There might be a few black sheep in the family. Lesbian grand-aunt. Playboy uncle. Wild-child cousin. The relation that became a gigolo and no one talks about. The other one that moved away and has umpteen kids. The one with the record for number of marriages and divorces. They are all parts of a painting of possibilities, their genes and yours might be the same, you might get it the same way they do.

Were you traumatized by the kids at school? If they thought you'd get laid at all, they tried to match you up with the only other Asian in your class. "You'd look great with Jimmy/Carol!" You were the funny man, the joker girl, the best friend, the class brain. Kids didn't flirt with you, you didn't flirt with them. Early copulation is for trashy white or brown or black kids. Anyway, by now, you've gotten over this. Maybe.

Put your hand to your heart. OK. Woman? If so, that's a bit harder. Women pick up reputations like a static-charged TV screen attracts dust. If you want it, you're going to have to be either more brazen than most people, or much more discreet. Women aren't allowed to want it, really. You're sexual without being aggressive, flirtatious without being hungry. You'll probably get it through the romantic route. Perhaps a careful negotiation with someone that you decide you like. Maybe you'll learn each other's bodies like favorite picture books you had as kids. Reading the same pages endlessly, making them dog-eared and worn. You lick the drawing of an ice cream cone just to see if it has flavor.

If you're a woman attracted to women, it might be easier. Tender. Nurturing. Meet your lover at a dinner party thrown by a mutual friend. Or at the fruit and vegetable co-op, the bookstore, the women's night at the gay club, a political meeting. Lesbians aren't outwardly as sexual as the ones in straight men's imaginations, but close those bedroom doors and bang. Baby, you've got it.

If you're a woman attracted to men. Well, men are nothing but trouble. Do you go for an Asian guy? Your parents might love that. You might even love it too, having figured out that for you, love comes from sharing histories, having things in common, understanding each other. Men are so inexplicable, why make it even harder by choosing someone from a different cultural background? Or maybe you just like that smooth skin and jet-black hair.

Do you go for a white guy? There *are* a lot of them. Do you have to avoid the ones that have a reputation for going for Asian women, the ones with fantasies of dragon ladies, geisha girls, anatomically flexible Thai bar girls? The ones your girlfriends pointed out to each other at university and said *watch out*. You go out on a date. You find it slightly suspicious that his favorite movie is *The Joy Luck Club* and he knows not to douse his meal with soy sauce. You'd actually find that cute.

Maybe somewhere down the line, you've already gotten it, but you want more of it. You're in a relationship but the heat has been turned down, past medium, lower than simmer, it's barely on at all. You can touch your finger to the element and not scald your skin. That could be the time for an affair, complicated and careful work like an advanced bonsai course: a lot of waiting, a bit of trimming, wondering if what you're doing will turn into the right form. If it does, good. You've got it. Dangerously.

Put your hand to your heart. Man? OK. What are you going to do? Who are you going to go for? How much do you listen to your parents anyway? Have you considered if you're attracted to people on the basis of their race? Do you go for Asians, whites, or others (see above)? Or does it not matter? How can race not matter? Your whole life, people have treated you differently because of it. How can it not slide over to carnal matters?

Did you absorb stereotypes? Do you consider yourself less handsome for the shade of your skin? The images of public figures that you've seen who look like you are classical musicians, kung fu masters and TV chefs. Why isn't Brad Pitt Asian? Why did you get stuck with this body that seems so slight in comparison with those other, bigger races? If Asian men are supposed to be so sexless, why are there billions of people in China?

Regardless of race or gender, if you want to get it, you have to know that you want it. Be confident. Be obsessed even. Not too obsessed, not so you start to leer and grunt at inappropriate occasions, but enough to observe what's going on about you, to notice what works and what doesn't work, when a direct approach is going to get you the prize, or when you have to be more circumspect.

Listen. If you really want it, maybe you should consider being a gay man. You'll have to contend with the same stereotypes and racism that straight Asians do and gay Asian men have a few of their own trees fallen across a highway in a storm when you want to get to Memphis. But yes, gay men can get a lot of it, if they want. It's an odd trade-off between the pleasure of the senses and social equality, but sometimes you take what you get.

If you want it, you might even have to make sure you're in the right geographical location. I mean, if you're in a small town in the middle of Canada or Australia and yours is the only Chinese family for miles, it's not like people are going to see you and think *va-va-voom.* They'll think: restaurants, laundries, corner stores. Or maybe they'll think: foreign, different, strange. You'll probably have to move somewhere bigger.

It's true. People get used to other people in larger numbers. For a city to love Asians (including love that's horizontal), there should be a lot of Asians. It's likely that in between that stage of one Asian family and a whole population, there will be growing pains. It may be best not to be there at that time.

It's like food, which is a good analogy, a shared vocabulary of appetite, satiation, sensory overload, indulgence. Say there's one crappy Thai restaurant, it can serve anything it wants to because no one knows the difference. Then say there are a few more restaurants, a bit of competition, a few more seats, more people familiar with lemon grass and fluffy catfish. Then suddenly there's a craze. People are wild for Thai food, they can't get enough, connoisseurs appear. Sometimes, it's just about familiarity.

I guess you could always just go to Asia to get it. I mean not only are Asians attracted to other Asians because they're surrounded by them, but that extra cachet, that smell of *Westernism* or *Norte Americanismo* might make you even more the center of attention. Be among your people, and be different at the same time. Have your cake, or custard tart, or Malaysian steam cake, or mango pudding. And eat it too.

If you're still not getting it, maybe you should lower your expectations. Or your standards. Become promiscuous. Tell people that the word *promiscuous* is going out of style and has been replaced by the word *prolific*. Is there anything so bad about it? As long as you're safe and don't get any nasty bugs and it doesn't interfere with your ability to love, really love, someone else. What's the problem?

.....

Or maybe cultivate a few new skills, some tricks that not many people know about. That something-up-your-sleeve look combined with a cultivated expression of mystery might just be that hook you need.

Or maybe you don't really care about whether you get it or not. And that's OK.

Or maybe you get it as often and as much as you want. Forget you ever read this.

.....

Surf

I'm thinking about the colors of tanned skin. Sunlight boring into the outer cells of the body and each body reacting individually, changing into different hues, all of them inviting. I like the way that tanned skin in the sunlight makes you want to put your hand on it, to rest it there gently and maybe coax back some of that solar energy into your own self.

It's ten-thirty, a good time to be at the beach, I could get fried to an angry red if I were to stay out too long at noon. I wince at the thought: the sunburn wheedling up to the head's feverish fatigue, the peeling a few days later. My friends in Sydney go to tanning salons. They're too rushed to go to the beach, or maybe it's too far to go. Most people say they can't tell the difference but I think I can. There's always a trace of ultraviolet orange. Also, the evenness makes one suspicious at a gut level.

A natural tan is best, really. It makes me think of food: honey, bran, chocolate. But I could easily think of elements: earth—brown shale, red sand, the tan shade of certain rocks, parched soil; or metal—copper, bronze, platinum, rust. Even trees—though the tint of a deepening orange maple tree is probably unknown in Brisbane, as would be the paper-thin bark of the arbutus tree, narcissist, constantly stripping down to raw green underneath.

I miss those trees sometimes, but I'd rather be here. You wouldn't find tanned surfer boys in Canada. Not like these magnificent packs of young men striding through late adolescence, the particular motion of the body when walking in the sand. I'm glad I made the move to Australia and I was surprised at how easy it was: the whole world calls out for experts in IT—*Information Technology* (who ever says it by the long form anymore?).

Not only that but I get to go to new places, not just stay in Sydney with its excess of men and attitude and beauty—*not that I'm complaining*—but hey, hey, Brisbane-Brisvegas (I don't know why they call it that). Welcome me with open arms. Show me something new in these two weeks. Plus, I'm making this a long weekend and taking Monday off.

It was a pleasant enough journey to this spot: a train from the center of town, a ferry, a short bus ride, a little walk from the road through some trees and now I'm on this really long, flat white beach on Stradbroke Island that goes on and on. Step out of reality for a second, and you can imagine it stretching out forever.

That's what I'm thinking as I breathe out and watch the salt dry on my body. I'm a bit winded from playing in the surf. The scenery is calming me. There are some cute gay men here: a posse just ambled by in two pairs of Speedos and one pair of designer trunks, box-cut. I'm not as fixated as some of my friends but my eyes did settle at crotch level in this case. Shiny sky-blue Speedos was well-packaged, the light color of the fabric revealed a good contour: big balls, it looked like. Black Speedos was harder to see, seemed like he'd tucked himself off to the left. The box-cut got my prize: through a geometric pattern on white, he had his penis pointing right up against his belly. I love that habit, and the shape that results. And it was fat.

A lot of the surfer boys are wearing board shorts. I'd complain that they're covering too much but it's not a bad look. Tight little waistbands slung low on the body. Hugging a contour like two hands touching at the wrists and forearms and pointing away from each other, stretched out, forming a wide shallow cup. And in the space of this cup is a beautiful alcove where tanned, muscular backs slope into the shorts and then jut out suddenly and modestly to round, tight buttocks. And these butts are ready. Ready to be part of a balancing system to stay upright on the waves, the long board underfoot and now a part of their bodies. A great big hard long extension.

Other guys are wearing wet suits. I don't mind them either. I like the thought of men, young or old, squeezing themselves into tight rubber like a cock into a condom. I imagine myself as a pair of arms, a throat—either embrace. They hold up both sides of their suits, put one foot in, then the other, shimmy it up so they can slide in their arms. I picture myself as that material so I can press against all parts of their bodies. Funny, I don't get the same thoughts when I see a man in a nice pair of jeans. Maybe I should.

I was just out in the surf. I'm not a strong swimmer and there's a sign warning about the undertow here so I stayed close to shore. It was hard to be far out. The strength of the sea rolling in on big constant waves: swells would lift me five feet off of the bottom and put me back down, a wave would break over my head and fill my ears and nostrils with salty water. I tried to figure out body surfing but I'm not sure Canadians are naturally suited to it.

So here I am, resting up on my shoulders, checking out all the cute young surfer boys through my sunglasses when Brian walks by. He's tall and lean with long rectangular muscles. His surfboard is in his right arm behind him so his silhouette is a chunky cross. He notices me looking, or senses my lust, or his gaydar goes off. Something. But he glances over, and with his smile I forget everything: my name, my country, my present location.

"Hi," he says, though it might have been "G'day." Whatever he says, it's in the most natural way in the world, as if he always talks to strangers, and there's nothing unusual about somebody checking him out—which there isn't, since with that kind of beauty, I'm sure it happens all the time. I look left once and right and no one else is watching him, or us.

"Hi," I reply because "g'day" would sound forced, too chummy, a colloquialism that doesn't quite sit right with my Canadian accent. No foreigner ever learns to say "g'day" here correctly.

He stops and I tell him I'm here for work.

"Nice work if you can get it," he snorts, but not in a cruel way.

It strikes me, while we're making small talk, that I hadn't considered the possibility of a gay surfer. Not that the two things would be opposed: homosexuality; balancing on a board in the waves. But my image of the sport was of young, virile boys filled with straight testosterone. It's ironic that I try to fight against stupid prejudices but hold them myself.

"What do you do when you're not surfing?" I ask.

"I'm a florist," he tells me grinning. I sense he grins the same way anytime he tells this to another gay man. "Stereotypical, huh?"

No. His physical charm is so completely original that the word touches me only a second before it flies off.

I could sit and talk for hours but he informs me he's starting work at one p.m. today and should be on his way.

"You ever surf? Picked it up in Sydney yet? I bet it's not a Toronto kind of sport," he comments and my silent half-shake of the head indicates no. "Do you want to learn?"

Yes.

No.

Not really.

I'm scared of sharks.

And the water.

Anything to see you again.

My eyes come out of a blur and I'm looking into his smiling eyes. I don't know what I've said.

"Right, then. I can't tomorrow. So, Monday? Ten a.m. You're willing to come out here again? I do all the time, it's worth the trip. I'll meet you near the public toilet and change rooms over there. I can bring you a board. A nice big flat steady beginner's board." He winks at me and walks off, that surfer walk again. If I ever had an Australian fantasy, this is it. If I didn't, this is it.

He arrives on time. I was early. I couldn't stay away.

Surf

.....

The first lesson is on dry land. I thought we'd be in the water right away, paddling around, but instead we sit on the shore. He's describing the waves to me, pointing out patterns and where you should paddle out, how you should ride across the whitecaps, never go in front of someone else, watch out for swimmers, not that they should be out in that area anyway. *Is this information important?* I'm having problems concentrating. When he lifts his left arm to point out to the surf, part of his chest pulls out from his body, like the fabric of a kite being stretched on a frame. It forms this sail bordering the hollow of his underarm, which I'm guessing he probably trims. The hair is neither bushy nor sparse. It's a dark brown bloom, one of these new Australian flora I'm trying to learn the names of.

"You'll have the board attached to your leg anyways, never panic, it's not so rough out there. You might not be able to stand up the first time, but we'll see how it goes, first you can just try to get the motion lying flat, then kneeling. We won't stay in too long today. You don't have a wet suit. I don't want you to get too cold. Or too burnt. Lotion?"

"Uh, right," I say. "Forgot." I take the bottle from him, a waterproof variety and SP36: he's predicting that Canadians fry in the Aussie sun. I slather the lotion onto my legs and arms, chest and stomach, self-consciously, then neck and face. He dips his finger in a small container and reaches out and paints my nose.

"Pink zinc. Gorgeous."

I hold out the lotion to him and can't even get the words out but he grabs the bottle, squeezes, and efficiently rubs it over the parts of my back I can't reach.

"More please. All over. Lower. Higher. All around." That's

what I'm thinking at least. I'd suggest forgetting about surfing but if surfing is why I'm here, I'll carry on.

"Um, um... You." I comment. It sounds like an accusation.

"Oh, I put mine on already. Let's go."

I can't even seem to carry the board properly so I'm relieved when we get to the water's edge. Then instead of getting in the water, he makes me put the board flat on the sand.

"OK. Last lesson. You've got to learn how to pop-up."

I look down at my board shorts. I didn't tell him that I bought them especially for today, and I hope that he doesn't notice. But I'm checking whether I've still got the half-erection from when he was rubbing me down. I could pop that up.

He looks at me curiously wondering what I'm doing. "You've got to be able to stand up in one clean motion. If you can't do it on the land, it'll be a lot harder in the water. You want to be able to do it without thinking."

I look at him, and the board, and the sand. "You want me to do this?"

"Yep." He seems serious.

"In front of these people?"

"In front of me."

"Uh, OK." I lie down face-first on the board, tense my legs, and then hop up and draw them underneath me. I end up with my hands in front of me as if I'm trying to catch a ball. He says it's fine for a start. I look around. No one is watching. I do it again. And again. The fourth time I lose my balance and fall over on my butt. He doesn't laugh, just shrugs, and the slight rising and falling of his shoulders sets off small ripples in the muscles in his upper body. I forget my task, or my role of a student, and just look at him. I must look like a fawning idiot.

"Just a few more times then."

My first lesson is a minor success. The waves are small but steady. There aren't so many people out in the water that I run into anyone. I mainly paddle around and try to catch the rhythm of the waves. I attempt to stand up and fall over. Actually, numerous times, but I manage to do it once. The wave carries me in so slowly that I soon tumble into the water. But I am proud of myself.

"Bend with your knees, not your waist," I hear as I duck my head out of the water and swim towards my board. "Keep your weight over your feet. Crouch for control."

He paddles over to me.

"Can I bend over with my waist after?" I ask hopefully. I'm not sure if he hears me.

I'm tired but I ask him if we can go to where it is a bit rougher. I don't want to surf. I want to watch him. "Just a few times."

He agrees. I paddle my board in the water, awkwardly, trying not to obstruct others, but wanting to remain out in the ocean, as close as I can to watch him. The waves look far too easy for him but I marvel at how someone so tall can remain so upright on thm. The sun above drapes small shadows on his long torso; his muscles shimmer like the sea below him. He catches one long wave and heads far off down to the east. I get the full view of his body. First: his torso facing me as he catches the wave, then the side of his body as he picks up speed and finally his long back as he surfs away from me. Every part of his form lustrous in motion, steely and strong, confidently travelling on his long flat carriage.

Even though I paddle in his direction, and he in mine, it takes a while to meet in the middle.

"Enough?" he inquires.

No. I could never get enough of you.

We exit the water. "I'm exhausted," I say, then add, "and thankful."

"Don't mention it." We're in the men's change room, and somehow we're alone.

"Hey, have you ever been back here at night?"

He looks at me quizzically.

"Or you know, done it here, in the change rooms, or even...in the surf?"

He takes his time in answering. "When I was younger, a few times, maybe. You know, it's not comfortable at all. The sand gets everywhere, the saltwater stings. Some of the beaches have pretty sharp rocks and you scrape your skin. Out here, there's just sand, nothing to lean onto. It's a bit boring. I know something much more comfortable." He leans over me and blocks a shaft of sunlight coming at an angle through the doorway. Even his shadow feels good.

His room. Spacious. Curtains drawn. Smatterings of dusk seeping through. The walls are white but clothed in shadows. His bed is covered in crisp white sheets. There is a huge bouquet of roses resting in a crystal vase in front of a mirror on a low set of drawers.

"Do you always have roses in your room?"

"I cannot tell a lie. I hoped you'd be back here today. They're for you."

"Not daffodils or lilies? Not Australian natives—not that I can remember the names of any of them."

"Well, you're not an Australian native." He takes me in his arms.

Height. Did I confess how much I like tall men? Not all the time. In fact, I kind of like all sorts of men. But a tall man will make you swoon just because you have to look up. Then the blood tilts to the back of your head. He leans over to kiss you. *Wham.* Hopefully he stops your fall.

"I'm going to take a shower first." His voice has some command in it. First roses. Now what? "You can relax in here." He enters the bathroom, which opens directly into the bedroom, and shuts the door.

I sit on the edge of the bed at first, and listen to the sounds of the taps and spray, the slightly echoey timbre of the insides of bathrooms. I'm both exhausted and raring to go.

When he comes out, he's wrapped his midsection in a white towel. I grip his sheets in my hands so I don't tackle him to rip it off.

"Your turn."

I'm quicker than him. I let it all slide down the drain: the last remnants of the ocean and beach, the day's lessons, the heat.

I come out and he's lying back with his head against the pillows, a long silhouette, his legs slightly parted and the space in between a long triangular arrowhead which I follow, dropping my towel on the floor and climbing on top of him. It's like finding the ideal place on a beach and lying down, the give of the sand below your body, and then it molds to you as you mold to it.

We kiss and kiss, then he leans forward slowly easing my back down to the surface of the bed. I swing my legs out from under me until they wrap around his thighs and then he is on top of me.

"Let's fuck," he says, and even in those two short words there's that Aussie accent that I love. Lube has appeared out of nowhere, wherever he keeps it, his arms were long enough to reach without me noticing. He squeezes some into his right palm and reaches behind him to smear it between his buttocks. I must look quizzical and he reads my mind. "No need to warm me up, I'm an expert at this."

I can't believe how still I'm managing to keep when my insides are waves crashing against rocks. There's a speedboat in my head but I'm breathing out and in, and shaking only slightly as he slides a condom onto my cock, which is as hard as it's ever been. Unwavering.

He straddles me kneeling and I can feel changes in pressure and texture as he lowers himself onto me in two short breaths. Then he starts to ride, slowly at first, up and down, his eyes are closed tight and his head thrown back slightly, like he's taking in some signal from a far horizon. His hands rest on the front of his thighs, every muscle in his body warming up, moving, joining into a rhythmic motion. He opens his eyes, and stares into mine.

I'm reluctant to look away from his long torso, the tops and sides of his thighs, but I hold his stare and see in it: pleasure, satisfaction, and desire.

He rides me and rides me, his torso twisting back and forth, side to side, he is balanced on top of me with a reckless knack for the sport, an instinct. Bouncing on a wave, he is surprising me with his intensity. The sight of him makes my mouth go dry just as the rest of my body is covering itself in sweat.

I am about to ask him whether his legs are tired and if he's OK but it strikes me that this is what he does: standing up, squatting, a position halfway in between. These are surfing muscles he's using.

I am gasping now too, and as he lifts his body up, he squeezes his anus tighter against the shaft of my cock. On the downward cycle he grinds against my pelvis and I feel the head of my penis jostling against his inner sphincter. I think we've reached as far as we can go, can the elements get much stronger than this? He leans forward, places his hands on my chest and arches his back so my cock slides out from him. He whips off the condom, tosses it aside, and lies on his back. He's already got a condom out and is working it onto his cock which is gorgeous and erect. He leans then grabs me and pulls me into a position where I'm kneeling above his head.

"Let's warm you up." I lose track of his progress with the condom and lube as I feel his hot tongue inside of me, thrusting up into my anus. I have to grab my balls and tug so I don't shoot, right then, all over his face. He rims me for ages then grabs my hips in his hands, and guides me down towards his cock. "I like the hair on your arsehole. It tastes," he licks his lips, "textural."

Then, without my thinking about it, he's inside of me. I'm not used to being fucked in this position but I like it. The best way to learn something is to watch someone who is good at it and try to do the same. I'm looking at his face, as well as his torso pumping underneath me, and superimposed is the image of moments before, him being fucked in the same position that I am now—my shoulders, hips, thighs are moving like his did. I think I'm getting the hang of it.

Not for long though. I've been excited too much, for too long. The wave forms, the white foam turning over onto itself. The curve of it rises pulling everything from underneath it up into the direction of the shore. My legs are getting too tired to hold me up. I'm only a beginner at this. I rest down upon his cock, grinding, rubbing. My hands reach out to grab the handles of his chest. My cum sprays in all directions. I arch myself over him as he grabs his cock and pumps, a few decisive times. One of my hands still resting on his chest, the other now next to his head. He turns his face, kisses my wrist and groans. Salt from one ocean mixes with that of another.

When we finish making love, we shower. Together this time. We squeeze into the shower cubicle—it is rounded actually, like a space capsule—and take turns soaping each other down. I get hard again, and take him in my mouth, my tongue and cheeks responding to his penis swelling with blood, softening, different degrees of firmness. We dry each other with big, comfortable, white square towels.

We walk into the bedroom again and I face him. His skin holding that quality of just being towelled down.

I tell him there is a square of his body I like. Not a small square. I stand in front of him and draw it in the air with both hands. I start between his pectorals, move my fingers outwards in opposite directions about two inches above his nipples (the nipples are the best part, the angels in the corner, the whole way the painting is lit) and two inches past, then down the same distance, and back towards the middle of his abdomen. He is so tall and long and lean that this square shows not his whole belly but just the top part. So: the nipples, the line of his chest underneath, the starting to soar division between right and left pectoral, and then these rectangles, one on top of the other. I picture a hunky bricklayer putting them into place, this wall of stomach muscles. If I was to traverse it, I wouldn't hop over, I'd gently ease the bricks out and replace them behind me as I entered.

This, I say. *This makes a beautiful picture.*

He laughs at me, a small gentle laugh, and gives me a hug, strangely nonsexual, kind of the same reaction you might get when you can't help yourself and tell your woman-friend's boyfriend how hot he is and he's cool about it and he even puts his arms around you.

He looks into my eyes, and I picture my perfect square as a photograph mounted on the wall of my apartment in Sydney, right in the entranceway so it would be the first thing you see when you come in.

I drop by his shop before I leave Brisbane, and there he is, looking so different, an efficient florist in a cool room. I'm looking for a phone booth that he can change in, back in and out of his surfer boy persona or his Clark Kent flower guy shtick: either one is fine with me.

"I'd buy flowers from you but I'd give them right back."

And right there, in the middle of his store, he grabs me and pulls me into his tall frame, and into a kiss, a subtle, long, two tongues entwined kiss that doesn't break, even when the tiny bell on the door chimes and a pretty young woman walks in with a mischievous grin.

"How 'bout I call you when I'm in Sydney next," he tells me and walks calmly behind the counter. I hear the conversation start and fade like the sea caught in a shell.

"Brian, Lily got a promotion at work, I'd like the most beautiful bouquet of flowers..."

And as I'm out the door, I'm surfing:

Light offshores, blue skies, and a thirty-foot swell. I'm driving into the shore, and am on it without even a wait. I don't even know how big the thing is, but I know it's the heaviest wave of my life and I'm gonna ride it. My largest tube to date.

It spits as soon as I'm inside it and I can't see a thing for the entire ride. The board is part of my body, I'd entered the zone long ago, and the long appendage beneath me is doing what I need it to do: holding steady, riding fast, keeping me upright, my knees supple and bent, my shoulders and arms sensitive to any changes in the ocean beneath me, balancing me out.

The whole time I have my eyes closed, going, "I'm coming out. I'm coming out." I am thinking myself through the wave, envisioning me exiting the barrel. And I'm making it. Riding the most powerful wave. Somewhere far below is sand and earth. But here, right in the middle of things is me, balanced at the most perfect and unique place beneath the water and the sky.

.....

Shoes

Sex with Charles wasn't the first sex I'd had. But it was probably the first sex I'd had that wasn't romantic.

It wasn't hard to notice him. There were so few identifiable gay men at my small university that we all basically knew each other. The other men on the campus were mostly sensitive straight boys, hippie kids, and lefty intellectuals mixed in with small-town rednecks and only a smattering of jocks, since the university's small sports program focused only on rowing and rugby.

Charles hung in the background of one of the gay cliques on campus. He had longish red-brown hair and a solid build, strong arms and chest. You could see that, even if you couldn't see the exact contours. None of us wore the form-fitting uniforms of gay men in the big cities, though occasionally, to be daring, our slightly more colorful (or slightly more fey) garments would have an extra shirt button undone, or the sleeves pushed up unusually high.

When Charles and I finally arranged to get together, neither of us was completely sure what it would lead to, and the planning of it was more with nervous energetic attraction than calm and cool lust. There was never a sly wink.

But by the time I had arrived at his apartment—his alone, unusual for a university student—I had some idea of what was to come. Still, I was in no rush, probably because I was still trying to figure out what I wanted. Was he boyfriend material? Was he sex material? How did those things combine and in what proportion?

I spotted a novel on his shelf. It happened to be my absolute favorite at the time. "You're reading this?" I pointed, obviously excited.

"Uh. Well, I was." He looked at me with a bit of confusion. "I couldn't quite get into it. Not much of a plot." He shrugged and it struck me that his voice was—not effeminate, what was it?—*nasal*. Slightly high-pitched, not girlish, but cloying.

"This is my bedroom."

Well, give it a go, I coaxed myself. I'm not here to talk literature.

We leaned in for a kiss, and managed, in that perfectly instinctual way, to tilt our heads in opposite directions, open our mouths slightly and to the same width and make contact, motors running, those thousands of muscles that make us smile and frown now concentrating on the pleasures of the mouth and tongue.

He wasn't a bad kisser.

We felt each other's chests and backs through our shirts. These days I'm like an expert at choosing fruit, squeezing and pressing at exactly the right places to find what I want at just the right ripeness. But then as an amateur, it was much more about patting and stroking, not even fondling; big hand motions, as if I were wearing thick mittens. He was the same.

He stopped abruptly. Leaned back, and lifted up his red rugby jersey over his head in one motion. I was disappointed that I didn't get to do this for him so I started to work on his jeans. He complied easily which made me feel awkward since I was still mostly clothed. I paused long enough without doing anything for him to catch on and undress me. Finally, we faced each other, mostly naked.

His body was softer than I expected. Puffier. I didn't know then how different men's bodies were from those in the gay magazines and newspapers I read. Nor did I know how to eroticize nearly any body: to focus on the personality of a bicep, respond to the alertness of a nipple; to find hidden strengths below different surfaces, to discover something sweet and dirty.

I looked at him and his shy, shrugging smile, suddenly noticed a shock of red pubic hair, and decided that touch was more pleasant than sight. I leaned in to kiss him. We ended up doing a horizontal, swooning sort of dance. We rolled over each other and messed up the sheets.

I went down on him: my mouth a homing pigeon; his cock, a home. He suddenly stopped all motion, breath more shallow, body stiff, his arms flat out beside him. His cock was quite nice really, a bit rubbery tasting, but of solid girth. But the rest of his body seemed lifeless. Had I killed him? Death by blow job?

He pushed my head away, whimpered, and came onto his stomach. He paused no more than a few seconds before leaning up, pushing me back, and sucking on my cock with a mechanical enthusiasm. It felt good but wasn't enough.

Frottage was one of my first and favorite sexual motions, so I reached down and pulled him up to me by his armpits. I rolled him over, rubbed away like a dog in heat, and came into the space between us, which was still wet from his orgasm.

That was it, really. I don't think I even stayed for a shower, preferring to do it at home. I made feeble excuses when he telephoned, and then felt so embarrassed that I could barely talk or look at him when we came into social contact.

What was so wrong with not having good sex? I knew deep down that I was treating him badly by avoiding him after our one-night stand but I tried not to think about it.

Three years later, my travels in Europe had started in Scandinavia. I wasn't making it explicit but like hoards of gay men, I had made my decision based on sexual attraction. Years later, a colleague involved in social research told me about his survey of gay men and holiday destinations. The reasons for picking them? The place where you find the locals attractive. Or: where you think you'll get the most sex.

I fitted into this more in a theoretical way than in practise. In college, the few Scandinavians I'd met were beautiful, both men and women, and the men had a subdued masculinity I liked, not to mention handsome Nordic faces. I was curious to see what a whole country of them looked like. What that would lead to was hoped for but not preordained. The sauna in Oslo had been the site of one fantasy fulfilled: a strong-cheeked, sun-kissed, hard-bodied Norwegian gardener. Sweden, however, had no gay saunas, and I would have to try my luck at the disco.

I'd showered and wrapped a towel around my midsection

when I called over to my host, a friend of a friend of my gay brother's, to recommend a place to go out to that weeknight.

"The club at the RFSL, that would be your best bet," he replied and a visiting friend of his nodded in agreement. "Oh, and by the way, make sure you don't use my towel, I don't want you to catch my crabs."

"Or you to catch mine," I retorted without missing a beat. His friend laughed with raised eyebrows and I'd gotten the effect I wanted, though in truth, I was just trying to be daring and older than I was. I didn't know what crabs were. I could guess, but I wasn't sure.

The club was huge: a dance space and bar attached to a huge lesbian and gay community center with telephone help lines, counselling, social groups, and HIV and AIDS workers. When AIDS hit the gay community in Sweden, the government guessed that the saunas were a factor. Rather than using them as a place for education, they moved to shut them down. Gay activists offered a discreet deal: build us a big, fully furnished community center and we won't complain.

So here I was in a place some considered a successful negotiation and others a cowardly compromise, looking for sex, and dressed badly, since I hadn't figured out that part of gay culture. I wandered around, trying not to want a drink since the alcohol in this part of the world was notoriously taxed. Bar-goers drank *before* they went out. The place filled up. I could see that the Swedes were slightly blonder than the Norwegians, and maybe a little slighter. There were attractive guys here and there, but probably no more than I'd find in a Canadian bar. It was just that the ones I desired here had a look which I could feed into fantasies of Vikings and

Norse gods and Swedish skiers and tennis players.

I felt foreign and inhibited, not quite knowing how to join into the crowd of men starting to dance. I stood on a balcony, overlooking the dance floor, and noticed a man beside me with dark hair, a complexion of cream, and soulful, sad eyes—I couldn't tell their color in the dark.

"Hi," I said and we started talking. Travelling is an easy excuse for conversation so I didn't have to worry about that.

Bengt's English was perfect with a slight accent. He worked in finance for a small manufacturing firm, and didn't like dancing much. I liked his shyness, his inhibition, and his face, which was probably quite typical for a Swede, but to me was storybook handsome. He lived on his own, in an apartment in a suburb outside of the center.

"Will you take me there?"

"Do you really want to come?" He sounded curious, almost surprised.

I replied with a gentle kiss and my tongue between his lips.

It was a cold car ride there, the heater struggling against the winter.

His apartment was simple and sparse. The bedroom was all white: walls, furnishings, bedcovers. Something about the combination made it simple and stylish rather than clinical.

Our bodies tumbling onto the bed were dark shadows.

We multitasked. Our kiss never seemed to break while we maneuvered each other into positions where we could take off each other's clothes. His skin was even paler than I'd guessed, drained of color; he looked for a moment as if he'd just come out from an ocean swim.

Now: naked. He seemed shocked when I went down on

him. Startled maybe. Scared? A foreign aggressor in his bed who'd ordered him out of the nightclub and marched him home. I glanced up and caught his eyes, wide open, looking down at me. I looked back at the view inches from my face, pubic hair dark and distinct against his light skin. He was completely silent.

When I paused and let his cock slide out of my mouth, we reversed positions. It was a vanilla world for me, not just this sex but all sex to date: I stuck mainly to kissing and oral. I'd rimmed and been rimmed, maybe had a finger partially inside of me, but fucking was still a foreign country.

Bengt's shyness in person had unfortunately also translated to shyness in bed. The blow job was adequate. How, I wondered, do some guys give such good oral, others mediocre, and still others—something about the shape of their mouths or teeth—made me ticklish and squirming?

I put my hands to various parts of his body: underarm, stomach, neck, inner thigh, arse. But he brought out the poor lover in me.

I was about to go down on him again when he gently pushed me away, grabbed his own cock and in a pace that gradually quickened made himself come: an efficient jump of an orgasm. His whole body shuddered for a second and his semen landed partially on his wrist and partly on his upper stomach.

I was not far behind him, having started to jerk off at the same time he did. I put my left hand on his right shoulder and when I came (also efficiently, no great eruption) I pressed my torso into his and finished us off with a kiss. I noticed again the whiteness of the room but the edges had become somewhat indistinct: we were floating on a cloud that was cool and quiet.

I slept the night in this color, a glowing ivory tusk in the dark, occasional neighborhood sounds of a lone car entering a quiet suburb with its ordered apartments sparsely furnished.

I awoke in some wonder at having been in a part of the world I hadn't previously, not particularly exotic but off the beaten track. Bengt drove me to a nearby metro station and described how I could get back to where I was staying.

A few weeks later, now in Italy, I could truthfully and knowledgeably joke about crabs. I now knew what they were since I had seen them with my eyes, examining one on the end of my fingertip with disgust and embarrassment. I didn't know if I had indeed caught crabs from my host—from his towels or beddings. The Norwegian gardener had been too long ago, I figured, but then there was that German...

Bengt had given me his address as we'd left his apartment. I may have been naïve (in fact, I certainly was), but I'd guessed that Bengt wasn't the type to have a lot of sex nor bring many men back to his apartment, and crabs, if he'd ever even gotten them before, were an unusual thing. "I'm sorry," I wrote, "if I gave them to you." And I was.

Duncan was a country gentleman. Not gentleman as it relates to gentry or wealth, but to manners and kindness and an old-fashioned conservatism. He didn't associate with the gay scene in Sydney at all and wasn't up to date with social or political happenings. He had some gay friends, some straight ones, but mostly spent time alone in a large, recently renovated house with a big leafy garden and a goldfish pond.

I met him through the Internet. It was slightly before the

Gaydar craze hit, an Internet meeting service that soon swept all of its competitors aside. At the time, I'd discovered "the Pinkboard," a community notice board on the Internet. You could stick up personal ads but there weren't any pictures.

I was new in town, and truthfully, I wasn't sure what I wanted. I fantasized about finding a gorgeous lover and boyfriend, daydreamed about hot, sexual encounters and thought that friendships with interesting, attractive men would not be a bad thing. But how could I word my ad or choose ads to attain these outcomes and avoid the overly desperate, the psychos, or even just the plain?

In that short month of hopeful e-mail exchanges and Web-surfing, I met Jed—strong and interesting but desperate to end the coffee; Ned—a man so misogynistic that I prolonged the coffee just to see if how long his nastiness could go on (forever, I learned); and Fred—with whom I went for a gym workout and whom I wouldn't recognize on the street. Ed, I actually ended up dating for a short time.

And then there was Duncan. What attracted me to his ad was that he was smart, established and well-travelled. His rural roots surprised me when I met him because I'd expected someone much more urbane. I felt little physical attraction but conversation flowed easily, and I liked his energy. I was lonely and I needed friends. We embarked on a friendship.

I did find one thing difficult. I generally don't see friends too often, maybe once a week or less. In this case, I was hoping to show that I wanted a friendship and not more, but didn't want to have to spell it out. So, I tried to limit our meetings. Unfortunately, he was unemployed at the time; nor did he have much of a social life.

Shoes

• • • • •

"When are you free?" I'd ask, and expect a reply like those of other new friends—a suggestion of a general time and time period like "later in the week" or "how about Wednesday or Thursday night?" Duncan however would answer: "Anytime." And he meant it, day or night, the only item scheduled in his week was a short course in computing on Tuesday afternoons.

We'd met for coffee twice, had lunch once, and gone to the movies once—over a period of a month—when I agreed to spend Friday afternoon with him and then see his house. I had a day off from the temp work I was doing. He suggested a walk that I'd never done from Bondi Beach south to Coogee.

As we walked side by side that day, I wondered if I'd become too fixed in my physical desires. He had a strong tall angularity that had its own attraction. When he spoke about something that excited him, his eyes sparkled. Was I so shallow as to not be able to recognize these qualities?

We walked through picture postcards: South Bondi, Tamarama Bay, Bronte Beach. We spent considerable time exploring Waverley Cemetery, new and weathered headstones overlooking the ocean, their shadows becoming longer as the day stretched into late afternoon. I had my camera and got him to pose as the head of a headless angel.

We were both tired by the time we reached his home, where he proudly showed me the large garden and fishpond he'd recently completed.

"Would you like some wine?" It was a bottle of red, maybe fifteen years old. I'd never heard of the vineyard but sensed that it was expensive, and would be delicious. "A friend gave it to me and I've always saved it. Might as well open it up now," he said with a grin. We sat on the couch with two full goblets and made the simplest of toasts looking each other in the eyes. "Cheers."

I saw ahead of me two evenings. In one, I would finish the glass of wine, have maybe half a glass more and bid him good-bye. He would offer to drive; I would decline, thank him for the afternoon and catch a cab home.

The other evening, I also saw before it happened. I inhaled the wine through all the chambers of my head, its old complexity and softness of flavor. I edged just a bit closer to Duncan on the couch. I hesitated, because in the end, I knew I was making a bad decision. Then I leaned over and kissed him, crying out on the inside, "Is it so wrong to feel lonely? To reach for comfort on a dark, quiet Friday evening in a new country in a different hemisphere?" I cringed at the tone of my complaint and to block it out of my ears took Duncan to his bed.

Do I need to say what happened? That not even the kissing was right? That while I had had sex with dozens of men since Charles and Bengt, none of those experiences assisted me now in raising the level of voltage in the room or creating electricity between us? That we both came and there was a sad smell in the air? That I considered staying the night, and thought better of it? I kissed him goodnight and told him I could let myself out, it would be easy to catch a cab.

We never arranged to meet again, nor even ran into each other. A year later, I met him at the gym that I'd just joined and that he'd been going to for a while. He didn't recognize me and I had to call out and approach him. He was polite. We had little to say to each other.

Shoes

.....

Months after that, I sent an e-mail to him—his address was still the same. I apologized for having sex with him and falling out of contact and for any confusion caused.

He told me he'd thought I'd been "working my way through Sydney." I didn't take it as an insult. But I was saddened. It was as if he thought that the only way someone would have sex with him was if they were having sex with everyone else. I made silent wishes for him: confidence, a lover, a bout of good and crazy sex.

What comes around, goes around. What you do comes back to you. It's not a bad set of ideas. I want to believe them and sometimes I really do. But in the end, I think it's a crock. You do good because it's a good thing to do, not because you expect some reward. And people who do bad things probably have bad things happen to them not as a direct cause-and-effect but because they hang around in circumstances where they're more likely to occur. So, I don't believe that moments that I'm ashamed of like the ones I've described need come back to me in a reversed form. But when I'm snubbed by men, or my calls aren't returned, or I feel a bit used or confused by them, as I often do, moving about in big urban gay cities in search of friends, frolicking, and fucks, I try not to be angry. I can put myself in their shoes.

.....

The Perfect Head

He looks like his genitals.

You know those men who are handsome in a nondescript sort of way? Solid features, perhaps a little square-jawed. Everything in proportion, and basically symmetrical. All so regular that it is actually hard to describe them to someone else.

He doesn't look like anyone. You can't say: oh, just like David Beckham or Robert Redford, Paul Newman or Hugh Jackman. If he looks like an actor, it's someone who doesn't make it into the top credits. But really, it's just looks. Who wants to go out with a movie star anyway? You don't want someone else to get all the attention, do you? To have to cater to that ego? Some actors choose their vocation in order to be center stage and they don't mind if the focus goes their way offstage as well.

You wouldn't say he's sexy, that there's something about him. There's neither a particular aura nor an unusual sparkle in the eye. No slight ski-slope shape of the nose, eyes too close together, eyebrows too bushy, cheekbones handsome in the right light but ghoulish in another. There are no obvious faults.

The Perfect Head

.....

But then, there are no obvious attributes. You'd probably say good-looking because everything is basically in balance.

He doesn't ooze and schmooze with a style and grace that translates into someone you can't keep your eyes off of. You can look away. And when you look back, he's pretty much the same.

He has two principal expressions. One is a state of attention: he's looking at you, bobbing his head slightly, a steady, unwavering glance, neither challenging, nor piercing. He's not trying to get something from you, say, find out that story about the ex-boyfriend that you won't share with him. He's just watching you and you don't have to guess if there's something going on inside his head that you don't know about. He doesn't daydream symphonies, nor plot mathematical proofs. On the other hand, you can't say "there's not a lot going on there." Because there is. There's just enough going on. And he's looking at you.

The other expression is one of not looking at you. He's looking off into mid-distance. Maybe he knows you're there, maybe not. He's unconcerned. He's not waiting for you or someone else. He's content to be who he is. You've had other boyfriends who practised disregard, who developed active ways of ignoring you either to make you angry, turn you on, or simply confuse. This contrasted with the ones who were needy, who wanted your attention. No matter where you were looking or where they were looking, you knew they wanted something—it was like a soft pulse at your neck whispering: *want want want*. What a relief to find such lack of complication.

If he didn't smell of anything, you'd notice. Not on a conscious level. More like a typo in a magazine that you don't actually pick up but simply feel something is incorrect. So yes, his scent is masculine. Corporeal. A body with blood flowing underneath its cover. With water and salt in different forms moving about at slow and quicker paces. He smells of life, simply. That's it. No unusual pheromones. Just the regular ones.

Isn't hair a strange thing? How it can go suddenly awry the older you get: sudden appearances of tufts in the ear, one long single hair from the aureole of a nipple, three that sprout around a mole? Then there are all the variations of crowns and caps: slowly going bald all over, or just the top of the head starting from the receding hairline; hair that starts to thin; curly hair that becomes curlier, or straightens. Like the rest of his appearance, he has a pattern of hair which is unremarkable. You don't really notice it because it seems to be growing in all the right places, and has a gentle medium weight and color, perhaps three years off from turning salt-and-pepper. That kind of color.

And the size of him. If you want to know. He's a bit tall, and a bit broad. Strong shoulders, and quite upright. If you tried to pick a sport, you'd have trouble. He's not a thick-necked rugby player. He didn't play American football. He's not tall enough for basketball. He's not lean as a runner, not short and muscular like a wrestler, nor *V*-shaped as a gymnast. Maybe he's a soccer player, a few years after he's stopped playing regularly, though he still gets together with a bunch of guys, maybe once a month to kick the ball around. So he is tough. If you knocked into him accidentally, it would probably be you that loses his balance. He's upright. Erect.

When you hold him in your arms, he's solid without being hard. There's give but not softness. Have you ever gotten in trouble for fondling cuts of meat in supermarkets? Wrapped tightly in cellophane, a big hunk of beef or pork, something that could be roasted for two people, maybe more. The color pushing out of the wrapper. The weight of it in your hands. Someone scolds you.

He's like that but unrefrigerated. You can grab parts of him with your hands, or you could embrace him whole. Thin men have a bony length about them; muscular men: nuggets of sinew and tendon. Men who don't work out, or are even putting some weight on: they can be bouncy. Puffy even. You can leave finger indentations in them. So, he's somewhere in the middle of all of those extremities. It comforts you to think of yourself wrapped around him in play or passion or just to rest.

All in all, he's regular. He's handsome in his regularity. You look at him and you feel comfortable because you know what you're getting. You sometimes can't quite remember what he looks like when you're away from him. But when you see him, you know you're home again. He doesn't threaten you with a hidden secret, a sleight of hand, a fancy trick at the end of the evening.

What you see is what you get.

.....

Why I'm

Why I'm attracted to redheads: For their reddity-red hair, in praise of readiness, to play connect the dots between their freckles, for the contrast between the colors of heat (glowing orange cinder-stick, crimson spark) and the water colors of green and blue eyes.

Why I still don't make a lot of noise: I can't say that I *discovered* masturbation because I think I was always playing with myself. I'm surprised I didn't get whacked on the head or slapped on the wrist with a ruler. Maybe I'm more discreet than I realize. But when jerking off became real, or at least messy and finite, I kept the door to my bedroom shut. With my parents' room down the hall, my pleasure was in the sweetest silence.

Why I hate small talk: Because I don't know. I really don't. I may have lots of reasons stored up over the years, and other theories. But live long enough and they all get disproved bit by bit.

I don't know why I'm not in a relationship.

I don't know why I've not had many.

Why I'm

.....

Why I'm a fan of Tarzan: Because of that loincloth. Because of the names of the actors who played him. Lex Barker. Buster Crabbe. Mike Henry. Because he was the sexiest thing on TV. Because I can still taste the summer Sunday afternoons, the blinds partly closed to stop the sun from robbing the images from the screen.

Mike Henry was my favorite. At each glimpse of him, my breath caught in my throat like a loaf of bread at the shapes of his muscles attached to every part of his body, the light dusting of dark hair across his chest, his abdomen. His straining thighs and calves as he clambered up a vine that hung straight down from somewhere just out of camera range.

I wished to be at the top of that fake rope.

Why I'm a top: I've never managed to enjoy being a bottom. Certainly I'm jealous of those who can be both. Even the word is better, not a clipped *top* or mumbling *bottom* but the aerodynamic whispering projectile of *versatile.* It's a quality I strive for in other parts of my life.

I've met lots of guys who don't bottom ("the sad song of when two tops meet"). And I'm sure, almost 99.5 percent certain, that they don't get the following responses when they state their position: *"Really?", "I'm sure you'd love it," "C'mon, it will feel great," "Are you sure?"* It *might* be because I'm a smaller man, and we like to believe a stereotype of big = top, small = bottom. And it *might* be because we've gone past that time in our history when it was expected that some guys are tops and others are bottoms.

But I'm sure it's because I'm Asian.

I'd be a much better bottom if the chip on my shoulder

hadn't displaced up my butthole. If you look closely (*I love to be rimmed by the way*), it has faux-Oriental writing on it, you know, the type where they make the strokes of the letters look like Chinese calligraphy. It says, "I hate being stereotyped."

Why I became a slut: It took a bit of practise, but I got there. Too many years of groping for romance and romantic groping and when I discovered gay saunas, I became graceful, I would get into conversations with men whom I never would have met in my regular life. I could play at being confident. I learned disappointment, patience and happenstance. Later lessons were in one-night stands, cruising in parks, and orgies: all good. Strange new worlds.

Why I'm politically incorrect: Even though I hate the phrase, the way it was stolen from us, and long for the days when we could tease our lesbian vegetarian friends ("lesbitarians") about whether they weren't being a bit too serious in wondering whether the people who'd harvested these sunflower seeds were unionized—even though I hate the phrase, it suits me. While I recognize that it's the heart that matters as well as kindness, a sharp mind, and some sort of intellectual-metaphysical-emotional attraction, it's overruled in an instant reflex (reflux?). I try to blame chemical reactions or at least my dick. But I fall stupid at the sight of a pretty muscle boy. Actually, they don't even have to be that pretty.

Why this works to my disadvantage: Because I'm not particularly muscular (though I've tried and *how do they do that anyway?*) and muscle boys gravitate towards each other and hang out in packs like wolves or lemmings or feral dogs even and more often than not, the men who spend that much time on their bodies don't have too many interests and a fiction writer really doesn't give them a big hard-on. Though if they are smart and have a fabulous body too it's even more obnoxious so I try to degrade them by stereotyping them as dumb steroidy beasts.

For some reason as well, in unusual proportions, when I click on their profiles on any of the many find-a-dick/man/shag/mate Internet sites, I find racist assholes (not the physical assholes which I quite like but more the imbecile species) who not only are looking only for other white men but say things like: "no Asians, no pretentious people, no geriatrics."

Though I know I should feel solidarity with older men facing the same rampant too-fat too-old too-short too-not-white kind of same discrimination, different forms, or even build an alliance with pretentious people who are suffering from anti-pretentious societal tendencies, at the time I just feel pissed off.

Why I'm lately amused: At big dance parties in Sydney, I've discovered a subset of pale gay men who are very muscular and prefer Asian men: they dance with or around groups of Asian men who fly down from Taiwan, Japan, Thailand, Singapore, Malaysia and other hot spots.

Unfortunately, most of these gay men being danced around are from another new subset of gay men at dance parties: the Asian muscle boy, which leaves me bemused since I find myself finally the right color but not having gone to the gym quite enough.

Why I'm not bitter: Even though I can't always attract these tasty white muscle boys, the Asian muscle boys don't seem to mind that I'm not as muscular as them. In fact, they kind of like me. I wonder whether this is because they were brought up in Asia and don't have this weird devaluation of Asian-ness that happens in places with a lot of white people. But I don't question it too much, since they flirt with me, and I them, and on the dance floor (lasers, lights, music); it's good to rub my hands up and down over so many variations of gym product, my Asian brother lovers, my lover brothers.

Why I feel bad: It does make me wonder, though, why I can pull Asian muscle boys and not white muscle boys. Is sexual racism as simple as that? Because Asians are Asian they're not as racist towards Asians. Surely not.

My shameful confession is that I champion the sexual attractiveness of Asian men (or basically any men that you've never considered before because you just think they're not your type, you've never been interested, or it just isn't happening). And yet I have to admit that while I find other Asian guys attractive and have had sex with them, it never reaches fever pitch.

I had sex with the most beautiful Thai man in Bangkok's famous Babylon sauna. I kissed his exquisite jawline, my hand on his smooth perfectly formed chest, and at the end thought, *If that doesn't do it, it's time to admit to yourself you like (some) white boys the best.*

Which is handy, I guess, since there's lots of them, at least in places where I've lived the last few years.

I know it's not a contradiction to like white boys, and like Asian boys too but less, and to work towards gay men being less racist in bed. But it's not as neat a package as I'd like.

Why I like wrestling: It was the only thing on TV (except *Tarzan*, see above). It's way better than any static Calvin Klein ads or porno magazines. It's the body in motion, hyperactive overgrown children, arms swinging every which way, somersaulting, cartwheeling, reeling, falling, getting back up and doing it all again. The muscles move, strain, shimmer in the hot stadium lights.

Gay porn flicks display a limited range of movement (in/out, out/in).

Swimmers and runners are beautiful in their own mechanical way: stroke, stride, kick, dash. But it's not the same.

Gymnasts, now they're pretty good as well. There's too much covered up though.

Why I feel sad sometimes: Last year when I fell in love maybe the most I ever have and we settled month by month into a deeper relationship, there was this period near the end of the time that we were together when my physical attraction for my boyfriend waned. I didn't understand how it happened. I still saw the soulful brown eyes; his solid torso that amazed me, his rippled back a mantle over it. But my work was heavy, I had some drama with family, I was tired a lot of the time. I thought of sex, and seducing him, and finding a space in the day for it, but the other parts of life took over.

It was not that I lacked desire: a pot of sticky glue that was stirred and wanted release. We'd talked about our attractions to other men, and Tony wasn't the jealous type. That my head would turn on the street wasn't a problem. What felt wrong for me was that my extracurricular lust got in the way of my normal sex life.

We watched porn videos a few times before bed. Tony would end up graciously making love to me, but my head was up near the ceiling above us, on the TV, somewhere else. The images didn't enhance our sex. They got in the way.

Months later when we'd broken up, I wondered if all my sexual freedom has tainted my ability to be with one person. If while I was playing the fields of sauna and stream, bar and street, fantasizing about my perfect knight, in fact he was slipping further and further away from me.

Why I'm annoyed: Just now, I took a break from writing this to make a phone call. See, two weeks ago I went to a house-warming party with a friend, Antoine, and some friends of his I'd never met. They were ex-boyfriends, Ludo and Greg. They'd broken up a year ago but were best friends. I thought that both of them were attractive.

It was Ludo I hit it off with, though. I found his face inspiringly handsome and the conversation flowed easily. I consumed many champagne cocktails. He went to meet friends for an all-nighter. I wasn't up for it, but told him to drop by in the morning if he wanted to. I know what it's like to want to cuddle up to someone after a big dance session, the party drugs slowly easing out of the system. He left, after taking my address and phone number. Not ten minutes later as I was returning from the bathroom, Greg dragged me into a bedroom, shut the door and tackled me onto the bed. His tongue in my mouth, I remembered that I was attracted to him too.

Why I'm

.....

"You do know I just gave Ludo my phone number?"

"Yeah."

"And that I invited him to drop by in the morning."

"Oh, he's unreliable. He probably won't come by."

"And if he does? Do you guys do threesomes?"

"Not anymore."

"So, if he comes by?"

"We'll go to my place instead."

Greg and I had a hot and drunken night but when we met up the next week and I leaned into him for a tongue-kiss, I was stopped.

"I just want to be friends."

Ludo didn't call me that week. He eventually sent an e-mail saying he'd spoken with Greg and was a bit shocked by what had happened. "He would recover"—a joke with a grain of truth—and I could call him if I wanted to in the next few days.

I left if for longer than that. I didn't feel that Greg had acted in malice but he'd certainly managed to make me feel uncomfortable about contacting Ludo.

I called him just now.

He said a cheery, "Hi," and not five minutes later, "I'm dating someone. I just thought I should tell you that. I met him last week." We maintained a conversation a little while longer before he said, "I don't think it's a good idea to see you now, but you never know. Sometimes these things last only a couple of weeks."

"You've got my number," I said, unconvinced, knowing that hooking up with both members of a former couple was never a good idea, that I'd left calling Ludo too late and that I didn't even know if I really wanted to get involved in something that became so complicated so rapidly.

That's why I'm annoyed.

Why I edit: Months after, maybe even a year after I wrote the main body of this story, I was back in Thailand on a business trip, in the same sauna that I usually frequent (see above, *Why I feel bad*). I met a gentle-faced Thai man who spoke not a word of English to me. We made love in a cool, dimly-lit cubicle and I felt an attraction and lust for him that I'd not felt so far for another Asian man. Note to self: retract painful admission above. Note to self 2: Have sex with more Asian men.

Why I was a comic book fan: I can remember my first superhero comic book. I was waiting for my father on an upper floor of an old tall and narrow building in Chinatown, the headquarters of our family association, one of the old clubs formed to provide support for the first Chinese immigrants. Membership was based on having one of the same last names as "The Four Chinese Horsemen." Although the implication was that these mythical men were our ancestors, I wondered if it was just an excuse to get together. The tiny shrunken friendly woman who lived in the building left me with a sugary drink and a comic book while she'd gone off to chat with Dad. I opened the worn and yellowing pages.

It told the story of a blind man, a lawyer, whose senses were so honed that he could fight, leap and throw his billy club in all manner of ways to save people who needed it and battle menacing characters. His name was Matt; he had red hair—(see above, *redheads*). When the corporate suit fell off, the change was miraculous: superhero muscles bound by a skintight suit of the deepest red, an acrobat tumbling into my young transfixed imagination, my obviously *gay* imaginings.

Many years later, I read articles in the gay press and chapters in books on gay subculture examining our obsession for the body beautiful. They posited that we have been over-influenced by a self-perpetuating ideal promoted in our newspapers and ads. Maybe with a broader range of images portrayed, our tastes would be more diverse.

Maybe.

But I remember that comic book and my initial attraction to it as something pure and simple, like the shine of the coin that appears under your pillow when you lose a tooth.

Why I can't understand other men sometimes: When we make love and they focus only on my cock (which, admittedly, I think is quite OK) or my ass (which I don't look at enough to pass judgment). Or they aren't wild about kissing, or have a limited range of motion. They must think I'm crazy, licking them toe to head and dipping into each ear, and fingering each part of their bodies like a musical instrument: an ancient cello with a sonorous tone. I want sex with each part of their bodies and in a dozen different rhythms.

Maybe this is to make up for the fact that I'm vanilla. Exceptionally vanilla with only a few sprinkles.

Why I don't mind bodybuilders: My friends, much more down-to-earth and politically correct in their desires than I, are nearly uniform in their rejection of men whom they consider too big. *Yuck. That's too much. C'mon, he has no neck.* While the same men remind me of the comic books I read when I was young. (See above, *Why I was a comic book fan*). I want to dangle off of their overblown chests like a rock climber, feet swinging in empty air, hauling myself up, hand over hand, to the most difficult and impressive overhang.

Why I don't write about love: I'm scared. I meet men. Friends, and friends of friends. At bars and through sports teams and all the different ways you meet gay men. The ones I'm referring to are the ones who are alone, and have been alone all their lives, never seriously dating, hardly having had a relationship, with nothing much to say in that conversational domain. I consider my history, count up my two significant but short relationships. I think about all the types of love I have: for my friends, family and life. How little experience I have with love for a lover. I think about those men and wonder if I will be one of them.

Why I'm not sure about rimming: What's not to be sure of? That most vulnerable pink flesh, a perfect aureole, an invitation to go further and just as much, the sounds of pleasure from someone who likes being rimmed. If he's got a gorgeous ass, it's simply beauty surrounded by more beauty. It's like being offered dessert. Do you always have it? Or do you need to be in the mood for it? Or are you not really up for this particular slice on offer? However, when it's right, it's right. Who can resist? Not too sweet. Maybe a touch bitter even. As extravagant or basic as suits your fancy. Decadent. Dig in. Stick your spoon in it.

My problem is I tend to get parasites and an accompanying whopper of a stomachache. Which can set me wondering what other unhygienic things I've been doing and pondering why I seem to get every single VD and bug out there—Hep A, crabs, warts, unspecified infections of the urinary tract—small detours on the road to pleasure; trade-offs when I didn't know I was trading.

Why I'm confused: After all that I've said, I have met many men whom I am attracted to who have good minds and hearts and forms. I do not compare them to the unrealistic men in my imagination. I try to be neither too needy nor aloof. I usually don't have to do much trying anyway, because when I click with someone, words flow easily and it's not difficult to be myself. But I'm confused that I meet these men when I'm not available or when they're not available or that when they are, I can't turn it into something that is more solid than a couple of dates. Then it's back to my life as a single gay man.

Why I see a pattern: If you can see it *(dear reader)*, of course I can see it! It does, admittedly, seem a little pat. All this childhood fantasizing (see above)—am I stuck in a Peter Pan stage of arrested development?

I have an excuse.

I was protecting myself. What good would it have done to have crushes on other boys, or worse, a teacher? What about falling in love with your best friend? What about other people being able to see your desires out in the open so they can be shot down like ducks in a carnival game? The prizes—the stuffed animals, the cheap radios—went to the shooters, I knew that. Better to live in my head, a quiet room of strongmen and daredevils. No chance of getting caught then.

Andy Quan

• • • • •

How helpful are fantasies? Or, not quite the opposite: are they not helpful? Which is not quite the same as: how harmful are they?

Live them out.

We can see that this is happening. Men with leather fantasies can buy a harness, go to the local leather bar, or more extreme, book a dungeon through the local classifieds, pay someone to dominate or be dominated.

People of all proclivities can find an Internet newsgroup or chat room for any particular desire: dressing up in large animal costumes, say, or squashing things.

I went to the local gay wrestling club for nearly a year (see above, *wrestling*) and though the novelty and physicality exhilarated me, it was not in a sexual way. After months of wearing a costume of bruises on my forearms, biceps and thighs, after two neck injuries and a muscle torn in my shoulder, I decided to give it a rest. My fantasy was better in a form not so real.

What I really fantasize about is being in a loving long-term relationship. How can I try that one out?

Why I celebrate: I have cared about many men. I have known good hearts. I have had sex with men who look like the ones I fantasized about before I ever had sex. I have had sex with men who look like anyone who I ever had a crush on. I have had sex with numerous men at the same time and it was fun. *Woohoo.* I celebrate sex both by doing it and by writing about it. I can write about my life believing that honesty is helpful, useful even, sometimes transgressive. I embarrass myself but don't flinch as much as you'd think.

Why I'm

.....

I celebrate because it's good to be appreciative.

And because pushing borders can lead you to the most wonderful lands.

And because there's still time.

.....

The Scene

It's not cold out, but it's cool for so much exposed flesh in the night air. The chill is offset by anticipation. I'm calm on the outside but heat is building up around my shoulders and jaw and through the top of my ribs. We've arrived, the three of us together, and my girlfriend. Tom all in black leather: a cap, a vest over his bare torso, pants, the ones that buckle up at the crotch with hooks. He's carrying a big leather bag filled with equipment. Jack is a step behind, subservient, wearing a collar, a white T-shirt and a jock under his leather jeans. I've got on what I always wear. Red handkerchief around my neck. A cap over my shaved head. Jeans. Leather vest, nothing underneath. The vest is heavy and hangs straight down from my shoulders. You can't see my breasts underneath.

It's the early nineties, before Inquisition moved into a bigger hall and the promoters opened up ticket sales to a couple of thousand people, not just practitioners but also voyeurs and tourists to the scene—which is OK since it lets people see new things and it's not as if you're going to force them to do a scene on their first night. But now, it's perfect: a smaller, more intimate crowd, hardcore leathermen and fetishists, dancing all night long at the Dome in a dark, round palace of pain and pleasure.

I'm pumped up. I've been waiting for this. I can hardly keep still while we're waiting for Tom at the bar. He's dropped our gear in the performer area. He walks by and people nod, everyone knows him. They lust after me, a dark, cute young boy, heavy eyebrows above my Maltese eyes, sex in my smile. Jack is this gorgeous Chinese boy, shaved skull shiny like polished stone, a perfect *V*-shaped torso. He doesn't meet the glances of others. He's ours tonight. I kiss my girlfriend good-bye and tell her I'll meet her later on. She's a bit nervous. She's dressed up real femmy with hardly anything on. The boys are treating her a bit funny.

"Hey." I grab Tom's attention. "When do we do the show?"

Even in the dark, I can see how blue his eyes are. He answers in his own sweet time to show who's in control. "We're not doing a show, Jos. We're just doing a scene."

Tom, my master, has been planning this for a long time. Maybe since the first time we met. My best friend Rodolfo had been telling me for ages, you've got to meet Tom. You have to. We met though without introduction. I was standing at the pool table at the Beresford, looking at this handsome leather-daddy, thinking, "Fuck, he's hot." When I see someone I like, I look at him or her from top to toe and then all the way back up. So, I'd noted his leather cap, hair beneath streaked with grey, the outline of his goatee and moustache, a strong torso, his arse, thighs, calves and leather boots. I checked everything out. *Sexy as.* He'd shifted around as my glance started its ascent, but I only got to his knees before I felt the pressure of his eyes on me. I looked straight up to his face: his head cocked to one side, tongue in one cheek, questioning with his bright blue eyes, saying, what do you want? He sauntered over.

"You must be Jos."

"And you must be Tom."

That was the beginning.

The party's filling up, it's getting on one a.m. and it's already starting to go off. You can feel it. There's going to be dirty, filthy sex here tonight. There's a scene starting already. I can see that's where we'll be doing ours. In the corner of the Dome, there are round rooms surrounded by Perspex glass. They call them the Meat Fridges, an explanatory name. They're back rooms with high ceilings, from inside of which you can see the whole dance floor. They've rigged up low lighting and curtains too, which are lowered down when a scene is being set up.

"Jack, look. There's going to be a flogging!" The curtains rise and you can tell it from the way the figures are standing. One is leaning against the wall, hands probably tied up somewhere; the other has legs slightly apart, arms out to the side. They've probably got a few toys out: pussy willows, whips, cat-o'-nine-tails. I can't tell if they're men or women. Who cares? They'll start light, little scratches; get louder; lay down careful practised strokes. Eventually, you'll hear the sound of flesh searing right through the Perspex. Someone's going to have a back that's purple and black for a whole week. *Wicked!*

Tom and I hung out a lot together. We'd go to men's sex clubs. He'd pick up boys and men and we'd go back to his place to play. He had this perfect, intricate setup with tiny hooks in the wall in his kitchen. Or we'd go to the bars. He'd sit or stand at the counter and greet friends or nod at new

•••••

admirers drawn to his handsome face, his confidence. I'd turn heads as soon as I came in. Shaved head. Leather. Denim. Flannel shirt. Full-on, saying, *yes, here I am, come and get me.* I wasn't trying to fool anyone. The guys, their heads would turn, they'd come to make a move for me, some would figure out I'm a girl and turn away but others I could see slow down or stumble, their steps tripping over their thoughts: *Does it matter?* They'd come and talk anyway and say, "Hey, I was coming to pick you up but I don't think so now." And I'd be like, *Why not?* Some of them I'd take home. Or go to their dungeons. I'd tell them first, "Look, I don't want your cock up my vagina. The rest we can negotiate." Then it was on for young and old.

Tom wanted me to meet Jack. He said, "I've got this slave, and I think you'd get on really well together." He arranged it. We went on a date. Jack right away slipped into slave mode and I was lapping it up. He could barely talk, he was so smitten. I'm really thin, drug-thin, barely have breasts. He liked that. And I could see that he was a dirty, fucking dirty boy. Just wanted to be defiled in as many ways as he could. He looked up, smiled, looked away. It was going to work out. Before we parted, he said, "Whatever we get out of this, whatever happens, I want you to fist me. I've never had a girl fist me before."

Jack looks relaxed now, calm. We're in control. Or Tom's in control of me, and I'm in control of Jack. Right in the middle. Where I like it. A balancing act where to stay upright someone has to hang on to your hand from above, and someone else is letting you balance your foot on his shoulder. Acrobatics.

An hour or two pass. Time goes quickly in a place like

this. The perspiration and music eat up the edges that would make a minute last longer. We head over to the Meat Fridges. I don't know what the previous scene was, but four men stumble out, flushed and tired. They stop near us. I turn and see a back covered in new shapes and figure they were doing a piercing, the kind that my friends and I like to do.

Usually, you attach these plastic threads to needles with metal piercings at the end of them. It's more like tubing. You put the piercing into the plastic, guide the needle and thread through the skin, remove the plastic and leave the piercing there, through a nipple or eyebrow or the lip of your labia. But we just put the thread through. They're different colors depending on the width. And then cut them off leaving thin lines of purple and black and red forming patterns on skin. We'd do it as part of bondage and domination, submission and torture, all pleasurable, and even more: *color-coordinated.* Shallow piercings, no blood, just through the top of the skin, no flesh and when you don't want them in anymore, you just pull them out. They heal with no scars. But when you've got them in—a *V*-pattern up the wings of your back or along your breasts—and you put on a shirt, no one knows. How crazy and beautiful you are when you're stripped down to the skin, looking like nothing most people have ever seen, human but with new spikes and spines, some new being.

It's our turn inside. We get out to the back. I'm all excited. Tom and I don't need to change. Jack simply strips down until he's got on nothing but a studded cock-ring at the base of his balls, everything pulled through. He's beautiful. Gorgeous face. Clear, smooth skin, taut muscles; stunningly built, a pliable sculpture. I have no idea what we're going to do except for me fisting Jack, but I trust Tom. He'll tell me what to do.

Tom opens his bag of equipment, and unrolls onto a table this fabric like a chef's knife roll-up with individual pockets. I can see metal shining but I don't know what it is. The rest comes out too. Tit-clamps, tiny hard alligator clips with sharp teeth, gags of different shapes and sizes, restraints. A bag of pegs.

"Get to work."

Tom grabs the bag and Jack stands in front of us, his arms out straight to the side and legs apart.

"Where do I put them?"

"Anywhere you want. Make patterns, do something beautiful."

I clip the first peg on near his wrist. It doesn't hurt much. It'll hurt when it comes off. I make a row up one arm and down another, along the tops of his arms, the middle. We make a pattern on his chest, up his legs and back, and even on his stomach and sides where there's little skin to grab. Tom does all the work on his cock and balls. Somehow he fits twenty or thirty on there. We dress him in exactly one hundred pegs. We finish and Jack is a wooden marionette, body parts clacking against each other, he moves slowly and stiffly so that nothing falls off. We leave him there, spread-eagle to the air, and set up a table behind him.

The curtain goes up. People gather around right away. Tom tells me that I must never walk in front of him or Jack, always behind so that the crowd can see what we're doing. The clips have been on a good ten–fifteen minutes by now, you can see variations of white and red and purple on skin glowing eggshell white under the overhead lights. Jack stands in a star, like da Vinci's Vitruvian man. I look out through the Perspex and all I can see is leather, flesh, hair, faces, piercings, chains. It's amazing. We pull the clips off slowly, one by one, carefully, without touching anything else. They're small gestures but everyone watching can see the tiny flutters in Jack's eyelids. Everyone can feel what he's feeling. The release from the pinching, the blood rushing back in, endorphins gathering, releasing. A searing, exquisite pain. We take off all the pegs, leaving till last the ones on his cock and balls.

We push Jack back onto the table that we've already set up with ropes and restraints. His arms and wrists are pulled under his back so his chest is open. We restrain his feet at the bottom of the table. I've tied a strip of cloth coming up under his chin to hold him down. And we start.

Tom has a table of drugs: poppers—amyl nitrate—a rag to pour it on and hold to his face. We start with tit torture, alligator clips on his tiny broad nipples standing high on his taut chest. Tom takes off the clips and replaces them with clamps. I replace the cloth strip with a collar and chains. Jack's head swings back slowly from side to side, then strains towards chemicals being offered that open and close his senses, that make him aware of everything happening but less aware of the unimportant. The world in summation: pain, pleasure, surrender.

Tom nods at me. "Knife."

Some people like to play with scalpels, but I think they're too sharp, too dangerous. You can cut too deep. But knives I love, and I've brought my double-bladed dagger. I walk behind Jack and Tom as I've been instructed to do, go to the table, find a familiar shining shape, and with the greatest reverence return. Jack can see what I have in my hands. No fear. Another inhalation of poppers. Then one careful small carving, a diagonal slit from below his nipple to the opposite side of his stomach, and a second one to match it and make an *X*. The cut so shallow it barely bleeds and six months later, no scar will be found. I add another slice across his chest in a *V*.

Tom orders, "Get the smallest sounds, the metal shaft farthest to the left. And the syringe. And the KY."

I return to the table. There's a range of highly polished metal rods, made of stainless steel I think. They're arranged according to size, all about the same length, a short knitting needle, but ranging in width from the size of a large needle to that of your little finger. They are curved strangely at the end with a tiny twist. I've never seen these before; neither have most people watching. Tom goes to Europe and the States a lot and brings back what he finds.

Tom starts to work Jack over; he fingers him and plays with his cock. He gets me to fill up the syringe with KY jelly and hand it to him. He puts a tiny dot of KY at the opening of Jack's penis. Then holding his cock loosely, Tom puts the tip of the syringe inside and pushes its plunger down about an inch. He strokes Jack's cock gently, puts down the syringe and I place the first sounds into his right hand.

Next, he squeezes Jack's cock with his left hand, and inserts the metal rod into the eye of his penis. He wiggles it a bit and then the sounds seems to just slide in by itself. Jack lets out a long moan like the reverberations from a huge copper bell. By this time, he's had this really tight cock-ring on for some time. His cock has become something else, different colored, different functioned. The three of us work together. Tom gives me orders, and I'm his assistant.

Get me a sounds two sizes bigger. Now.

Work his nipples. Put the larger clips on.

Put the ball gag on.

I put the ball into Jack's mouth and secure the gag tightly around his face. He can breathe and moan but he can't talk. Tom withdraws and inserts wider and wider sounds, plays with Jack's butt then tells me, "Go glove up. I think it's time that you fist this little boy."

The crowd can see what's coming each time I return from the table and I hold each article up as if I'm a game show hostess. I pull on a long, black rubber glove. Ceremoniously, I open the new tub of Crisco. *Shit!* The glove is too big. I'm swimming in it. *Tom, fuck, the glove is enormous.* It's a glove that fits him but not me. He smiles gently. I grab onto the end of the glove with my other hand, and try to yank it further up my arm, hang on to it so I don't lose it.

I don't bother with a finger at a time like I'd usually do to warm someone up. Jack is already warm. He's so hot, he's burning. Our eyes meet. He doesn't need to talk. I know he's encouraging me. *Go! Go!* He's ready. The drugs have loosencd his insides, his outsides. My hand made into a fist goes in easily, even as I'm hanging on to the glove with my other hand, wondering what the look on my face is.

Wonder, I think. I've fisted women before. But cunts are way different. Vaginas, you can only get in a certain way. They can open up like a balloon inside, and that's what it feels like, a balloon, you can feel around but you can't go any further. Once in full arousal, the walls suck back, your hand inside a magical sphere.

But this! Before tonight, I've never gone so deep, felt these different stages and parts of anatomy. I push up and through. Jack is open to pleasure, to me, to vulnerability and a physical connection that few others will ever reach. I'm inside him, not with a part of the body that urinates or comes, but with my fist and hand, which I use to feel the world.

Tom is still playing with the sounds. I look over when he takes one out, and it's amazing, the eye just stays open, looking out, it doesn't close up. He puts in the largest one, and while Jack is writhing in pleasure and pain, the end of the metal shaft is vibrating and floating around, like a long extension of the penis. His cock is purple. Small and shriveled from no oxygen

Before, I'd only wanted to be a top, but I'd gotten to the point where I wanted to try both, to be in the middle: someone under me and someone over me; to be controlled but have the liberty to do what I wanted to someone else, to do whatever I wanted with a body but at the drop of a hat, be completely subservient—up and down, changing roles, switching spaces in my mind. Playing with my boundaries.

Time has passed, maybe forty minutes since the curtains went up. I've been inside of Jack maybe ten or fifteen minutes. It's time to stop. I slowly withdraw my hand. Jack shudders and his anus closes shut like a door. Tom lets me do the last work. I untie Jack, and help him sit up. They let down the curtains. There's no applause but even through the walls, you can hear lusty voices, excited, amazed, shocked.

.....

I'd been so absorbed into the scene, I'd forgotten that anyone else was out there.

We pack up, wipe up the blood, make sure Jack is OK. He looks high and bright. Soon, he'll put on a G-string and he and Tom will be dancing for the rest of the night. I'm amazed that after such intensity, he could be one of a crowd. But that's what we showed people tonight. What the body is capable of. The mind too. We could have been you. You could have been us.

Moving out from behind the curtains, I thank my master and nod to my slave before we split apart. Tonight we were part of something completely new, and also, very very old. I'm shaking and so buzzed that soon I'll have to find my girlfriend, leave the party, go home and fuck. I pass a girl in the crowd, someone I know, a leather-girl. Her eyes go wide and I can see it click: she thought I was a slave-boy too, just like everyone else did. I think she's impressed.

It's enough. I don't go to another Inquisition for seven years. What could ever match this night? Me with my favorite master. In between him and a hot slave. Jack getting fisted by a girl for the first time. In front of rough men in leather who didn't even know that I wasn't the boy they were desiring. I was more than that. Sex, and something beyond it.

• • • • •

Just a Small Orgy

What better way to ring in the New Year than an orgy? Is this what the ancient Romans did, or just what we like to think they did? While I've been to many of the parties thrown by the Heavenly Orgy Team (HOT), I've never been to the annual one on New Year's day. This is because instead of being held in Sydney, it's organized eight hours up the coast, in the warmer clime of Byron Bay, an after-party to the Tropical Fruits party in Lismore, the country New South Wales version of a big gay dance party.

I'm staying at the home of my friend Anthony's boyfriend. Anthony used to live in Sydney, and he used to come to HOT parties with me—once or twice we even volunteered to help at the door together. But a year ago he fell in love with Julian, from Melbourne, who owns a house near Byron. Anthony has no regrets as he drops me off at the party. "I don't need anyone else besides Julian," he tells me and it's neither bragging nor advice. "Call me if you have problems getting home."

I'm curious about this party but nervous too: it's a bit remote and there will be less people. If I'm not enjoying myself, it will be hard to leave. Maybe there won't be the choice that there is at a big party. A beautiful man from Brisbane whom I'd met in Sydney, but not had sex with, had told me he'd be here, but then cancelled at the last minute.

I walk up through an area where cars are parked to the side entrance we'd been alerted to. It's a holiday home—rented just for the occasion. Just through a bamboo gate, there is a walkway made out of paving stones and a lush, compact garden. It's so tropical in this part of the country! A young man in the corner is undressing, and as I move towards the covered back porch, there are more men in various states of undress.

"Welcome, welcome!"

I spot Tony, the president of the organization, at the welcome desk.

"Glad you could make it. Did you enjoy the party last night?"

Since he reminds me, I can see that it is the day after the night before. Some men haven't slept at all, and others, like me, have managed to get only a few hours. Echoes of different songs are still running through people's minds. Some shuffle to an unheard playlist. I relax my shoulders, which I can feel were tensed. It's hard to feel uptight when everyone is so mellow. There is a group of men sitting in a semicircle while some are inside already, fully naked.

"Drinks are out here. You know what to do. Have a good time!" Tony grins widely. I figure out that I missed his welcome speech since I don't hear one later. I spot people that I know, nod and wave. Ask them how their nights were.

I look inside the sliding doors and step into an entrance foyer with a dark room off to the right, and a bathroom to the left. Off to the right of a large room in front of us is a bedroom being used for tonight's clothes check. There is a small kitchen off to the left blocked off with a mattress turned on its side.

The action has already begun. A group of four in one corner are starting a scene. In the middle, a young guy is bending over with his hands to the ground and his arse straight up in the air. A generous offering. I wish I could do that. Touch my toes. I'm not very flexible.

Others are pairing up, but mostly there's milling around. Maybe twenty guys in all. Like the motion of musical chairs where everyone shuffles around in random patterns, unsure of how quickly to move, whether to bunch up or remain alone, and when the crucial direction will be given. I'm not quite warmed up yet, and watch from the side. It's a fairly young group. I'd guess that the majority are men in their late twenties and early thirties, a slightly younger crowd than in Sydney. There seems to me to be a flourishing of strawberry blonds, at least four or five in the crowd; their hair shines through the dark and picks up color from the dim lightbulbs. It's an attractive group of men, even though, at the moment, I don't feel particularly attracted to anyone.

I'm tired from my lack of sleep. I move slowly, enter the mood of the party like someone who hates to jump into a swimming pool or the ocean, the sudden change of temperature and shock to the system: warm to cold, dry to wet. I am actually worried about my lack of interest. Who do I think I am to not be attracted to so many good-looking men? Why do I always set my sights so high? Isn't that just a natural setup for disaster?

Case in point: dark, slim, and handsome—a sculptured, taut body with long, gentle curves over hard muscle. His torso, especially his abdominal muscles, is defined with soft and hard lines marking gentle indentations or protrusions. I always write on lined paper, refuse the plain white stuff. I like divides. Guidelines. Ways of making order. Like me, he is not joining in but stepping into waves of men that part and close around him, none touching his skin. I've learned at orgies to be assertive. Waiting for a signal could mean missing the train. It could even mean missing the last one for the night. Stepping aboard to check if you're on the right one is just fine. It's not necessary to ask first. If it's the wrong one, you'll know.

I find myself next to him. I raise my hands together reverentially and touch the center of his chest softly, then move them out to the sides of his hard pectorals and then down inwards towards the xylophone of his stomach. I've unconsciously traced the symbol of a heart. His skin is cool and perfectly smooth. Many men on the scene shave, but I think this is a man who really does have a hairless torso. He doesn't look at me but instead over my shoulder, at other men, at a group scene in the corner. Yet, he doesn't move away. I lean my head down, extend my tongue and lick upwards from his stomach so I catch the overhang of his chest and flick his nipple—a small oval protrusion—from the underside.

Mmmm... I actually have to close my eyes and pause to savour what happened. Taste and touch stirred together, a pinch of vision. A nice combination of the senses, I think, and as I open my eyes, he's moving away from me and into another part of the crowd. As beautiful as he is standoffish.

I decide that this slow pace might just suit me so I step towards the porch to take a breath. Outside, I spot the shape of someone, and then as the features become more recognizable, I feel a hot burst of lust hit me. He's sitting down and in this position, his muscles are sort of bunching up on each other, even his plump cheeks and wide face seem like muscles from here. He has a different kind of muscularity than the man I was savouring inside. That one brought to mind a statue from ancient Greece, cool and classical. This one outside is hot-blooded and fleshy. He looks like a roast beef dinner. He spies me watching him. I catch his glance but can't hold it. He doesn't look like he has any intention of moving.

I decide now I really am horny though it hasn't increased my desire for anyone in particular except maybe the god. I make eye contact with a few others, exchange some touches and squeezes. I nod at some men that I know. I come across the statue-god again, and he actually pauses in front of me. This time I feel with every part of my hands, and draw them both down, palms flat outwards against his skin from his shoulders to his groin. I try to memorize the shape of him with my hands, think of them as electronic, drawing in signals that I'll be able to play back at a later time.

I drop to my knees. He's semierect. This part he shaves. He's left a bit of hair around his cock and balls but the trimmed quality is a nice match to the sleekness above. I take him into my mouth, in and out, smoothly, not too quickly. If he's looked at me even once, I've not noticed. He is still unengaged, and proves it, sliding out of my mouth, and walking away with a smooth glide and shuffle around me. It gives me enough time to get to my feet and not look as if I've been left there (I'm tempted to use the train analogy again). It doesn't feel hostile but is mystifying. I wonder if I'm really going to enjoy myself at this party.

Just a Small Orgy

.....

It's friends who come through in the end. At least, it feels like we're friends. We have mutual ones at least, and I've always liked Fearghal, his growling northern Irish accent, and the slightly long features of his face. I'd never noticed quite what a nice chest he has, strong and round. We've nodded at each other a few times, looked each other up and down, but now we stop, facing each other.

We kiss and fondle and I can feel his amusement, which I share, that we know each other already. We embrace, simply holding each other as motion continues around us, quieter and then faster. There seems to be a hot scene building up on one side of the room: a tall, handsome aboriginal man is fucking a strawberry blond, who is leaning over and groaning with pleasure.

Fearghal and I have grabbed each other's cocks and we push them against one another playfully, the head of his into my balls, my erection now circling around his.

"They're the same size," he says, and I wonder that with so few words his accent makes them sound so different.

I notice he's right. "Yours is a bit thicker," I comment, "but otherwise exactly the same." An Asian cock. An Irish cock. Twins from two races.

After such a long buildup of excitement, it doesn't take us long to both arrive at orgasms, standing up, facing each other, leaning into each other, kissing, and finally, ejaculating.

"Thank you," we manage to say at the same time, and then laugh.

There's only cold water. All those men. All those showers. A finite hot water tank. I sponge myself down with a wet towel. I decide to leave some of the smell of sex on me. Who's going to notice? And if they do, they'll know what it is. Maybe it's what they're looking for.

Outside, I take a break, sit on one of the benches and chat with new friends. Andrew is from Brisbane, handsome and fair, a solid forty-year-old. I hope that he'll go in for sex but he never does. Maybe he's just here to spectate. Winston is sitting next to him. He's from Kuala Lumpur and has a solid, slim muscular physique. He's an animated conversationalist. I see an empty seat beside the muscleman I'd admired earlier, and manage to slip into it without looking too calculated. Roast beef. I clear the thought from my head. He doesn't really look like roast beef. Or does he? I introduce myself. He's Sam, a graphic designer from Sydney. He and his flatmate have hosted HOT parties at their house. On Calispel Street near the beach.

"I think I've been to that one. Are you the guys with the cats?"

"Yeah, that's us." And I remember a view of the water, and the frantic motion of cats trying to find places to hide away from the action of the party.

"I don't remember you there." And I don't, which surprises me since tonight, I find him so noticeable. "Aren't you ever going to come inside?" I ask. "I've been hoping you'd go in."

He allows a small smile, then pretends he didn't hear the last part of my sentence. "I'm not in the mood yet. Maybe I'll go in later. Maybe in a little while."

I grab his knee gently, and use it to push myself up to standing. "OK."

I go inside again but Sam doesn't follow, and I can't see anything I want to be a part of. Fearghal is locked in an embrace with a young redhead. The group seems smaller. Maybe there's another room being used. Sometimes, these orgies just don't have enough sex. In and out. In and out. But it's just me moving back and forth between the porch and inside. Not the in and out I want. I give up and decide to stay outside for awhile.

A couple approaches. "Hey, we've met before," says the shorter, more fair one. "I'm not sure where."

"Fred, it's Dougal's friend, Warren." Davy turns to me. "You're Dougal Whitman's friend, right? The writer? I'm Davy and this is Fred."

I recognize the names but I don't remember meeting them.

"New Year's Eve. The Pride Party."

"But that was the first night I met Dougal."

"Ah, but we remember you. You terrified him."

I do remember them vaguely. I'd spotted their friend Dougal, walked straight up to him, kissed him on the lips, fondled his chest, and then disappeared into the crowd. Which might have seemed pretty regular for a dance party, but unlike most of us, including Davy and Fred, Dougal doesn't do drugs.

"Yeah, we thought you were cute. We were encouraging him to follow you."

"Well, it's nice to meet you finally," I say.

"Nice to meet you," says Davy and Fred drops to his knees. I have an erection that I didn't notice before and he's sucking me off. My brow furrows slightly but I continue talking to Davy. It feels great. I'm not attracted to Fred, but I don't mind the sensation. Maybe it's karmic. Other men have allowed me to find pleasure through their bodies while not attracted to me. Why shouldn't I return the favor to someone else? Why not be generous?

So Davy and I chat with each other while Fred converses with my dick. We decide that for Dougal's sake, whom none of us have told about HOT parties, we'll say when we see him that we met at the party last night and not this one. I find out that they're staying in my direction—probably the only ones who are, since most men are staying south of Byron in different hotels and cottages. I ask if I can get a ride later so I don't have to ask Anthony to come and find me. Davy says it'll probably not be a problem. Fred reemerges from my nether regions. I put my hand on his cheek and nod.

Then Davy and Fred do that thing that long-term couples do. They sense each other's next movement, and follow step without any verbal communication. They've started moving towards the door before they explain, "See you out here. We're going to have a little look inside again."

I'm left alone momentarily and decide to grab a beer from the ice cooler. I notice who is next to the ice cooler. It's the tall, dark, aloof man from inside. My statue-god.

"Hey," I say and finally he looks right at me. Black eyes. High cheekbones.

"Hey."

I introduce myself, and he does the same. "Ari." It's as if nothing has happened. It's not as if he's pretending not to recognize me. It's how it is. We are drinking an icy beer outside. Inside, I was sucking him off. We are surrounded by men. And it is an orgy. To master an event like this, you think of the present. You can also edge into the near future. But the past (even if it's only five minutes ago) is past. Savour it, dissect it, regret it (but hopefully not) after the event.

Tony passes by. "Fisting show in room number one," he announces. "Fisting show in room number one." There's only one other room in use besides the main one, so we can all guess which one it is.

"Eeee...," comments Ari beside me.

"Eeee...," I agree. I tried it once and might try it again but public demonstrations make me squeamish.

The ice is broken. Finally. A semblance of a smile on his face. "How was your New Year's Eve?" I ask, and he replies in a comfortable, deep voice. We chat for the next five minutes until he excuses himself to go inside. I chug my beer. Maybe alcohol will help. I don't think I can leave now. I'm not sure how I'll get home if Davy and Fred don't give me a lift and who knows when they'll be ready?

I stand and wait and begin to think that it's a bit chilly to be naked and outside when finally (finally!) I see Sam the muscleman (beef) rise from his chair and head inside. Of course I follow.

The dark room to the side, where I suppose the fisting show has taken place, is now packed. I'm guessing it's a bedroom with the furniture moved out of it. It's very dark. You can hardly move. Men turn to find their way out of a cul-de-sac, a dead end, the corner of the room, and are blocked by a leg, by an arm, by a threesome, by a foursome, by someone down on his knees, and another one on his back, and one on top of him while another waits his turn. It's like Twister, but not as fun. Or a lot more fun, if you happen to be in the middle of it and that's where you want to be.

With one step, I move to the edge of the crowd and my nostrils fill with heat and moisture and salt. My skin touches the skin of others as my eyes adjust to the light. I notice Sam only a few bodies away and I lean in that direction to see if the current will take me there. It does and I find myself in a circle-jerk of four or five men, all handsome in different ways.

Sam really does have an unusual body. Smooth like Ari's but with a completely different texture, a fairer, more Anglo-Saxon paleness. His chest and upper torso are big, the shape of a uniformed American football player, the fabric of the jersey capturing the width of the shoulder guards above. It's a hard body too, there's little give to the muscle and skin. But at the same time, every part of him, from his face down to the melons of his arse, looks overinflated, a tire that you're afraid might burst, a carry bag that you've crammed to capacity. I reach over across the circle with my free hand and touch his fat chest with as much wonder as lust.

With my other hand, I've grabbed the cock of the man next to me, and he does the same to me, as he also seems to be doing with the person on the other side of him. He looks at me (he's young, I'm guessing midtwenties, boyish, with dark blond or light brown hair) and we tilt out heads slightly in opposite directions and kiss. His tongue is warm and full, and I focus only on him for the moment, crawl into a small dark space like an intimate hiding place. This is what I've been looking for. Feeling desired while I'm desiring. Reciprocation. Which is all going pretty well for everyone by the sounds of it: a rough, jumpy curtain of energy building up through moans and grunts. Sam has a look of concentration about him as if this task is the key one. Must succeed.

It's all too much for me. Only a few minutes have passed but the anticipation and waiting from before seem to have balled up. The man I'm kissing is sensuous. I get a ridiculous pleasure from my one roaming hand skirting up and down the bodies of the other men in the circle, squeezing one's balls, stroking the shaft of another. Most of all, my fingers on Sam's comic-book muscle. He really is the center of the energy, having drawn all of us to him. My breath is catching on itself rhythmically. Three short groans transfer up from my throat to my mouth and I know that the man I am kissing feels the sounds in his mouth too. I come.

It's not like gay porno movies where they've managed to get all the actors to come at the same time—or at least edited it to look that way. I'm the first to blow, and I don't want to detract from the others' energy. I take a deep breath and a step out of the circle, which reforms like water rushing in to fill the space of something removed. I make my way to the washroom, but there's a line. I wait, sticky, with the others, a shared joke on our faces.

Two orgasms in one night is enough. I decide it's time to go and sit down on a bench outside on the veranda. A tall, enthusiastic man, who I recognize as one of the volunteers, is on his knees next to me going down on a tough, muscled man with a goatee—handsome, extremely handsome, in fact. I try to picture whether he would be as handsome without the facial covering. "Yes," I think, as I watch his face slide into different shapes of pleasure. The thought of reaching out and fondling his chest crosses my mind but I hold back and give them privacy. There is moaning and sucking, eyes rolled backwards into the head, and intense concentration on rhythm and suction. The tall one presses up from his squat and puts his hands on the shoulders of the man sitting.

"Thanks for coming. You have a safe trip back, right?" He pulls him up into an embrace and it becomes clear to me that the seated man is ready to go and his partner has been sitting next to him on the other side of me. He's also gorgeous. They make noises of leaving, and head inside to gather their clothes.

Phew! is the sound I think the tall man makes sitting back down next to me.

"He was hot," I try not to sound jealous.

"Oh, Matt? Yeah," he replies without being smug. "I met him at the party last night and convinced him and his boyfriend to come along."

"Good job," I remark and introduce myself.

"I'm Travis." A wide smile across an unusual face. Slightly goofy features. A pierced eyebrow. I find him neither unattractive nor attractive but like his unrelenting cheeriness.

"Excuse me," he says then leans down, his long torso crossing the space between us. His mouth on my cock. I can now relate to Matt, feel what he was feeling, maybe some bit of pre-cum, residue from his sweaty cock is now on my member as well. I rest my left hand gently on the top of Travis's head while he gently works up and down my shaft in such obvious pleasure. I'm happy to oblige as the party thins out, men entering and exiting the glass sliding doors of the house, empty beer cans and plastic cups being tidied.

.....

He lifts himself back up into a seated position. "Thanks," he says with a crazy grin. There's a lot of thanking going on at this party.

"See you." I stand up and kiss him on the forehead and go inside. There are still a number of men there but the lights are already on.

Wazza, the host, crosses the room naked but a phone pressed to his ear. There are ripples of laughter as men figure out what's happening. "Yes, fine, fine. Happy New Year. It's been good. I just have some friends over."

I spy Tony, who crooks his finger to me and explains, "It's his mother. He can't get out of talking to her. He answered his mobile thinking it was someone else."

"Of course, Mother. The weather's been hot, perfect." He's managed to cross the gauntlet of naked men, some of them fucking, and go into a room, one that hadn't been open for the party, and close the door.

Groans of pleasure among those left behind. Sexual. Or glad that it's not our mothers calling.

The party isn't winding down just yet. There are still men in the dark room. I go take a look. It has mostly cleared out. The thought hits me that it was more pleasant when it was crowded enough not to see the floor now strewn with paper towels and used condoms. But my eyes adjust to a wild commotion in the corner and I see that it's Sam, at it again. It really did take a while for him to get warmed up, but once he does... He's fucking someone with a piston-like action, motions hard and feral. He's on his knees and the muscles of his upper thighs and buttocks ripple with each slap of his groin into another man's arse. I recognize him too from earlier in the party. What an amazing bottom. It's a perfect match.

The bottom is on hands and knees but beneath him is another man on his back, his head underneath the bottom's cock, sucking his balls or shaft, I can't quite see. This man is jerking himself off, his hand near the face of the bottom, the action a tiny echo of Sam's fucking. Around this trio are more men, one fondling Sam's arse, two more jerking each other off but standing close to the others, to the motion and heat of the scene. A rhythmic beat can be heard, steadily, and suddenly, Sam throws his head back and roars, his jerking motions echoed by the whole group: six toy soldiers winding down. Unfortunately, Davy and Fred are the last to leave. They're insatiable. The main room is completely empty. The volunteers wearing shorts and rubber gloves are picking up condoms, wiping up lube, and cleaning off the mats that were laid on the floor. Davy and Fred emerge from the coat check and duck back into the dark room. Fred flashes me a sheepish grin. I'm wondering if there is anyone still left in there. One or two? I change into my clothes, and help clear things that look touchable. Finally, Davy and Fred emerge with the other last man standing. Shower quickly. Change. Good-byes to the organizers and cleaner-uppers. We're finally out, and exhausted.

As we drive up the highway, we pass a man walking up the side of the road. I turn back to look at him. Fred asks, "Is he cute?"

"No. Well, actually yes, very, but he's someone from the party. Can we turn around and offer him a lift?"

We swing around and go back, turn around again and pull up beside him. It's Sam the muscleman. He looks extremely startled. I remind him, "We're from the party. Do you want a lift? It looks like a long walk to town."

"No, that's OK." He shakes his head but still looks distressed.

"Are you sure? Where are you going?"

"I'll walk." And he starts to.

I stop him. "Do you need to use my mobile phone?"

"Oh, yes. Please." He finally looks at us with an expression of trust. I hand him my phone and we wait inside the car.

"I wonder what's going on," comments Davy.

Sam hands the phone back through the window and I ask, "Are you OK? Do you need a lift now?"

He finally feels some obligation to explain. "It's my boyfriend, Ari. I lost him. He left early without telling me, and he's got the keys to where we're staying."

"We can drop you off."

"No, he's coming back to pick me up."

Feuding lovers, or maybe just miscommunication. It finally clicks: Ari is his boyfriend. The dark god from ancient Greece who didn't seem to be having that much fun at the party has driven off, leaving the beefy sex god wandering around in the middle of nowhere. I recall the command and intensity of his fuck earlier this evening. Then his helpless lost-boy face of indecision. The two images don't match up. But I've offered help, maybe too much kindness. We leave him where we found him, trudging along in the gravel next to a ditch.

I wake the next morning in a daze. Julian is up with a first cup of coffee.

.....

"How are you, tramp?" he inquires.

"Good," I reply. "Happy New Year."

"Anthony's still sleeping," he gestures towards the room. "He'll be up soon to hear about your adventures. Were they good?"

"Oh, not bad." I tell him. "It was just a small orgy."

.....

Six Positions

I'm making love to the oldest man I've ever been with, his hair is white as Egyptian silk, his skin is translucent, blue and pink, I can see his heart beating from excitement. I am drawing an arrow down with my tongue, shoulder to opposite hip, a ribbon of saliva like a banner from a beauty pageant. This one says, "this man has tasted and been tasted by men for decades." Blood ricochets around his body and builds at his surprising erection. The wrinkles on his face, arms, hands, so loose, a multitude of scrotums all over his body, which I take up into my mouth like dinosaur eggs, rare plums, a tulip's head unopened. With veneration, I lift, squeeze softly, hear a gasp like an ocean caught in shells. It is the last ocean. It is wet. The tide recedes like sadness.

I'm making love to the fattest man I've ever been with, his anus cannot be found amidst the mounds of flesh, but his mouth, pink, red, puckering, surrounded by two round cheeks, has a passing resemblance. He laughs a great thrusting belly laugh the whole time we grapple, him turning and flopping, me dodging the weight whirling all around for my own safety. Every part of my body is a phallus, my fingers, hands, arms, legs, head. I press these into skin that says, yes! and takes me in, out, in, out, sweating, sliding, surrounded by warmth, by darkness. Somewhere in this maze I find a cock that is fat and round like a root vegetable. I punch at it, grasp it with my hungry hands. Hear a voice as if outside of a room or all around, of god, or a pregnant mother, "*huh huh huh*." The sticky fat flood smells of appetite.

I'm making love to the most exotic man I've ever been with. He has eyes like jungle animals. Tigers, wildebeests, possums, crocodiles, sloths, night owls. His skin turns color depending on the angle of light: dark as petroleum, as the center of your skull then yellow as the eyes of jungle animals—tigers, night owls, crocodiles. As slight as a bamboo reed, then a tight round muscularity on fire with bound up strength. Then two breasted and big cocked and more pictures, pretty pictures, so many I'm almost blind and I fuck him I fuck him I fuck him until I am covered in the fluids of my own exertion, thigh muscles, stomach, arms, still tensed, energy hanging on me still. Shivering, and when the thought returns to my head, I understand him not a bit more.

I'm making love to the thinnest man I've ever been with. He is so thin and long that he is sharp. I bleed with pleasure. He places his fingers down on me and leaves a lovely symmetrical arc, five small half-moon-shaped pricks. The air on these incisions feels spiny like a cactus, a tall spindly one with a downy white veil of spikes. Like pins and needles, when a part of your body has fallen asleep, and you have to shake and shake to get the blood back in. I am in a desert of sensation, so quiet that every grain of sand is noticeable. But I do not notice as he clothes himself head to foot in rubber and enters me from behind. I don't know if it's his penis, his arm, his leg, his whole body. I just remember he's thin. It's suddenly an Arizona night and the stars are twinkling in time with an orgasm soon to arrive. Sensation pours through the star-holes, the rest is black. Each time I exhale, one of the stars goes out.

I'm making love to the smallest man I've ever been with. Small is beautiful, he has attached his mouth to my cock, his legs dangling down, I feel ENORMOUS. He leaps and lands on my tit, bounces on my nipple like it's a trampoline, does cartwheels and somersaults up my stomach, around my neck. My touch on him is crude but large; he rubs into it like a cat, then returns to my crotch where he gives special attention to each square millimeter. When he finishes the last, I explode. I worry I've drowned him, but he shakes himself off in a triumphant dance, slides down my leg and disappears.

I'm making love to myself. Really. With elasticity and extra parts. I am seeing what all the others have seen before me, I am tasting my nipples, which come alive and harden, punctuation marks in the air all around me. My voice. *Oh oh oh*—periods. *Uh uh uh*—commas. *Awuhaaahh*—question mark. Gasping hyphens, sighing slants, I grunt out underlines. I am writing myself onto my page as my cock extends long, so long, I'm entered. I'm thrusting into myself. I have ten hands. I have eight tongues. A line between my balls and thigh. The slit in my throbbing head. A dimple where chest meets abdominals. All fingered. All stroked. All tongued. The skin of the page curves into its wet stain. Words run into each other.

Acknowledgments

With thanks to previous editors and publishers of these stories: I appreciate your fine work to help shape them into the form in which they appear in *Six Positions*. A special nod to long-time supporters James and Richard. A toast to small presses! Gratitude to all involved in making this book—including Kevin for excellent editing and Andrew for bringing these words to more people. Also, to anyone who's ever inspired a lustful thought in me: *gracias* for the inspiration.

About the author

.....

Andy Quan is the author of *Calendar Boy* and *Slant*, and the co-editor of *Swallowing Clouds: an Anthology of Chinese-Canadian Poetry*. *Calendar Boy* was a Lambda Literary Award finalist. His poetry, fiction and erotica have appeared in numerous publications in North America, Australia, and the United Kingdom. His erotic works have been featured in eight of the *Best Gay Erotica* series as well as in *Best American Erotica 2005*. After living in Toronto, London, and Brussels, Andy currently resides in Sydney, Australia where he works for the Australian Federation of AIDS Organizations.

• • • • •

The following pieces were previously published as noted.

• "At First Sight" was previously published in *Best Gay Erotica 2000,* edited by Richard Labonté.

• "First Draft" appeared in *Best Gay Erotica 2003,* edited by Richard Labonté and *Best American Erotica 2004,* edited by Susie Bright.

• "Getting It If You're Asian" appeared in RICEPAPER Magazine V7.3.

• "If It Sticks Out" appeared in *Quickies 2,* edited by James Johnstone.

• "Instrumental" appeared in *Carnal Nation,* edited by Carellin Brooks and Brett Josef Grubisic.

• "Positive" appeared in *Best Gay Erotica 2002,* edited by Richard Labonté; *Positive Nation,* April 2003, Issue 89; *Best Gay Asian Erotica,* edited by Joël Tan; and *Best of the Best Gay Erotica 2,* edited by Richard Labonté.

• "Rufo" appeared in *Boyfriends from Hell,* edited by Kevin Bentley; and as "Love Gone Wrong" in *HQ Magazine* June 2002, No. 91.

• "The Scene" appeared online at www.velvetmafia.com (issue #7); and www.lustre-magazine.com.

• An excerpt from "Shoes" originally appeared in *Quickies 3,* edited by James Johnstone.

• "Six Positions" appeared in *Quickies,* edited by James Johnstone; *Best Gay Erotica 1999,* edited by Richard Labonté; and *Best of the Best Gay Erotica,* edited by Richard Labonté.

• "Something about Muscle" appeared in *Law of Desire,* edited by Greg Wharton and Ian Philips and *Best Gay Erotica 2004,* edited by Richard Labonté.

• "Surf" appeared in *Best Gay Asian Erotica,* edited by Joël

• • • • •

Tan and *Best Gay Erotica 2005,* edited by Richard Labonté.

• "Why I'm" appeared in *The Love That Dare Not Speak Its Name,* edited by Greg Wharton.